Bitch, Please! It's Ivydell

Indie Sparks

Twice Shy Publishing

Thank you for escaping
to Ivydell with me
throughout this series.

I hope these characters have made you
feel welcome and that you will return to
them whenever you need an escape.

Ivydell will always be real in
the pages.

It means the world to me that you gave
these quirky little books a chance!

xoxo,

Indie

Jensen

When One Door Closes

IT'S EASY TO FORGET from one festival to the next how it feels when we open the gate. There's always a line of cars, and they're all just so damn happy to be here. I'm reminded again today how well I understand the feeling. Even during times when I didn't remember what happy truly felt like, I knew I was glad to be here, that here was better for me than anywhere else.

Shadow says he's always hated the way these people come to look at the freaks who live in the middle of the desert, to take pictures of our aging casitas and dirt roads for their social media profiles. I never saw it that way. Probably because I understood being in awe of it.

It's definitely not the kind of place I ever imagined myself living, but I'll always be grateful I got the chance to live here.

This year's festival is heartbreaking for most of Ivydell's residents, but it's bittersweet for me. I'm sad that Ivydell has to end, but for the first time in so long, I'm excited about my future. I was always going to move on at some point.

Ivydell has meant a hell of a lot to me, but now it's given me more than I could've hoped for. She didn't come here looking for me, and I sure wasn't expecting her, but Ivy Dell McAdams matters to me in a way I never thought another woman would.

Smiling, I wave the next car through the gate.

I turn to wait for the cars to move forward enough that I can let another one in, and I see Ivy walking away with Josephine and Zara. Her hair is on fire in the early morning sun, whipping in the wind like flames. She's flailing her arms as she talks, throwing her head back to laugh.

Just Ivy.

The cars are creating a traffic jam inside the gate as they stop to read the big sign that Petra insisted that we put up. It explains that there are fewer artists here this year. And that this is the final festival. Most of us were afraid it would kill people's moods to see the news, but the sign ends with a note of thanks and encourages everyone to enjoy the festival to the fullest. Nobody has exited the gate yet, so I guess it hasn't ruined anyone's experience so far.

Petra hasn't shared her plans for the future. I never thought she'd be someone I'd worry about, but losing this place will be harder on her. She's spent practically all of her adult life here.

A horn honks a few cars back. Cujo jogs back to talk to them. He's wearing a new leather vest. Plain. No patches. It's been a few weeks since I've seen the old one. I don't ask about the change, but I damn sure wonder.

He returns with two cold bottles of water. "They're worried about us standing out in this heat."

We both laugh. It's nowhere near hot yet.

The next car is finally able to drive in, letting another pull up beside me. A woman leans over from the passenger seat, stretching across the man behind the wheel. "Is it true there are rattlesnakes here?" she asks.

"It's true," I say. "But they don't want to be around us any more than we want to be around them. You probably won't see one, but if you do, hold still. It'll probably move on. There are safety signs posted everywhere. You'll see plenty of less harmful wildlife. Prairie Dogs. Chipmunks. Horned toads."

"Gila monsters?" she shrieks.

"No. Two entirely different lizards. Horned toads won't hurt you. But they're a protected species, so don't touch or try to pick one up."

She's already back in her seat with her phone in front of her face, no doubt trying to confirm my claim that horned toads and Gila monsters are not the same. Next, she'll doublecheck my claim that horned toads are protected. You can just tell with some people.

"Enjoy the art. Respect the desert." I wave them into Ivydell.

Welcoming people is not such a bad way to start the day. I'm sure looking forward to welcoming them into my winery.

My winery.

Life takes wild turns.

Ivy
Artists at Work

Josephine leads us into Myrna's casita. It's been transformed into a studio with jewelry on display everywhere. Zara stands behind a couple who are looking over the signature Wild Love collection, the pendants that include the one featured in the logo.

I smile as I watch my friend pretending not to eavesdrop. She's fascinated by all these people who are drawn to this arts festival in the middle of nowhere.

A stack of posters on the counter catches my eye. Can't wait to see what Myrna put on a poster . . .

It's a festival poster, but I know instantly that this is Josephine's art. Her style is unmistakable. Plus, I see the same rattlesnake that she tattooed on Cujo. Myrna walks over and nods. "It's perfect, isn't it? She captured everything that should be on our final poster."

"Are you selling these?"

"No. She's made us a poster every year since she came to Ivydell. Pays for the printing herself and donates them. We usually sell them, but this year, she insisted we give them away."

I want one, but feel guilty taking one from the visitors they were made for. Myrna notices me eyeing the stack. "She has one set aside for all of us, but you can take one from here if you want an extra.

There are more in every studio."

Josephine smiles when she sees us talking about the posters.

"I think Mom might want one of these."

"Then take one for her. This is it, doll. Our last hurrah. Get it before they're gone."

There is no sadness in her voice, just truth. This is it. I take a poster for Mom, and one for Zara, too. Holding it up to show her, I mouth to Zara that I'm going to put them in my casita.

It's weird to see strangers walking across my yard. As I'm unlocking my front door, a man calls out, "Are you opening?"

"Oh, no. I'm not an artist, just putting some things away."

The guy nods and keeps walking.

"How do you live here if you're not an artist?"

I turn to see a young girl, maybe thirteen, staring at me. She's walked closer, and I recognize the look in her eyes. It's wanderlust. God, I had it bad at that age. My little beach town felt so small. So boring. I knew I lived in a place that other people only got to experience on vacation. But I also knew I was bored out of my mind all too often.

"I just showed up." I laugh. "Actually, my mom lived here until she was about your age, and I always wanted to see it. So, I decided to spend a few months here."

"Wow. You just decided to move here for a few months, and did it?"

"Yep. You can do that someday. Just decide what you want and do it."

The glaze of awe that comes over her face makes me smile. I wish someone had told me at her age that I'd have that kind of freedom someday. It's not the same as being told that you'll be able to make your own rules when you're grown.

I think I needed to know that all my choices would be my own, not just that I wouldn't have a curfew or could use whatever words I wanted. Being told specifically that I could go wherever I wanted—*live* wherever I wanted—might've been good for a girl like me.

It might've warded off some melancholy to know I'd be able to just pick up and go someday. That I didn't have to stay where I was born forever. That I could uproot any time.

Maybe that's what I want now. To uproot and plant myself somewhere new.

"Can I see inside your house?" the girl asks.

I look around for her adults, but I don't see anyone looking for her. "Sure."

Leaving the door open behind us, I let her look around at my little temporary home while I lay the posters on my table. "This is it."

"But, how do you live here? Where do you work?"

"On my computer. I'm telecommuting while I'm here."

"Oh, yeah. My dad does that a few days a week. I just never realized you could do it from somewhere like this."

"You can do it from anywhere you want. It's your life. You get to choose."

"You're so cool. I want to be like you someday."

"You'll be way cooler than me." I nod toward the door. "I need to catch back up with my friends. And I bet someone is going to be looking for you soon."

She rolls her eyes and smiles. "Yeah, they'll be texting any minute to keep tabs on me."

"It's good to have people who love you enough to keep tabs on you."

I relock my door. "I'm Ivy, by the way."

"I'm Shiloh."

"Enjoy the festival, Shiloh."

"Thanks. Enjoy your life, wherever you go after this place is gone."

"Thank you. That's exactly what I plan to do." A hawk soars overhead, and we both look up to watch it. "Enjoy my life."

Zara meets me at the edge of the road. "Who's the kid?"

"Her name's Shiloh. She's bored."

"She'll outgrow that."

"All too soon."

Josephine joins us. "Want to go see what's going on in The Circle?"

"Yes. I've been dying to know what goes on there."

There is a steady stream of people on the path, taking pictures of everything from the prairie dogs to the safety signs. The wind blows, weaving a fresh herbal scent between us.

"I love that smell," I say.

Josephine inhales. "Wild sage. There's nothing else like it. I'm going to miss it."

"Doesn't it grow in Albuquerque?"

She shrugs. "Yeah, but it's not the same as smelling it here."

I know what she means. Nothing is the same as here. But nothing is the same in any one place as it is in another. It's easy to take things for granted when they become familiar, but when your time somewhere is limited, things become distinct, uniquely associated with that time and place. It doesn't matter if they exist somewhere else. It only matters that they are a part of this memory. Right here. Right now.

I hear a clanging sound in the distance. "What is that noise?"

"That's Shadow's hammer." Josephine smiles for a visitor who is taking her picture.

It seems rude to me that a stranger is taking her picture without even asking if she minds, but she doesn't seem to, so I guess it's fine. I think I'm starting to see Shadow's point about all these people looking at Ivydell like it's a roadside attraction.

"What's Shadow hammering?"

"He's a blacksmith. He opened his forge for the festival. Says he might as well show it off before he leaves it all behind."

"I didn't know he was a blacksmith."

"Yeah. He doesn't work as much as he used to, but he's good."

"Ladies! Can I get a smile?" The voice is coming from my left. It's some guy with a camera, who has ignored the signs and wandered off the path. He clearly wants to take our picture. Josephine and Zara huddle close to me. I want to flip him off on general principles, but my friends are already smiling. I'm outnumbered, so I smile, too.

The photographer jogs toward us. "Great shot! Thanks. I'm happy to send it to you. Can I get an email?"

I give him my work email. Seems like a better idea than giving him my personal contact information. He taps it into his phone and gives us a thumbs-up before he heads off to find a new subject.

Tawny is painting in The Circle. So is April. This is my chance to see what she paints.

"I guess Leo is probably handling his and Tawny's studio, but who is watching April's while she's out here?"

"Everyone doesn't stay in their studios the whole time," Josephine says. "Some of them come out here for a while so people can see artists at work. They leave signs on their door saying when they'll be back. In busier years, there would be a rotation of artists out here."

Zara sighs. "Man, I wish I'd known about this place sooner. I would've loved to have seen it full of artists."

"Yeah," Josephine says. "But all the best people are here for the end."

She glances toward April. "Well, they're mostly all the best, anyway."

"I almost feel sorry for her," I say.

"That's because you're too nice for your own good," Zara says.

"That's not true. Sometimes, I'm a judgmental bitch."

She and Josephine both laugh. They veer toward Tawny. I head straight for April.

I know she sees me coming, but she pretends not to. There are a few people watching her paint, and a few more looking at the finished paintings she's set on display around her. I quietly step closer to look at them.

Wizard? That's all she paints? Her cat? To be fair, he's a gorgeous cat, but how vast is the market for paintings of a giant silver cat? There is one of him crouched near a cactus, watching prairie dogs. In another, he's lounging in front of the fireplace in her casita. She's done one of him walking down a dirt road that looks like he's walking right at me, like he could jump off the canvas into my arms.

I guess if that one guy could get famous painting blue dogs, maybe April can be known for painting Wizard. I'm no art critic.

The painting she's currently working on shows Wizard standing on a rock with the wind blowing his hair. His eyes are piercing. If cats had romance novels, he could be a cover model.

April's work is so different from Tawny's. Definitely two different sets of potential buyers. I'm Team Tawny all the way, but I hope April sells some paintings.

I join Josephine and Zara, and we watch Tawny paint for a while before Josephine suggests we go see what Shadow is making.

Petra

Happy For Now

For the last time ever, my casita is full of festival shoppers. I watch a woman smell one of my mint soaps. She makes a thoughtful face, sets it back into the basket, and pulls another minty bar. When she smells the second one, she smiles and nods like she's found the one. I'm sure the tags have different scent names, but they are the exact same formula. Ivy's marketing genius at work.

I smile as I mingle, happy to answer questions about my oils and tinctures. I'm glad they're all here, but I'm glad to be leaving soon, too. Never thought the day would come, but I'm ready to live in a place with modern plumbing and wiring, a real garden, and a new greenhouse. It's time.

Winds of change . . . yeah, I hear you, Patty. I know.

Hell, I might even get a TV. A little dog to sit in my lap. It's never too late to drop back in, I guess.

I'll have neighbors in the traditional sense.

Goddess, help me.

The soap sniffer brings me two handfuls of items to tally up for her. My urge to just give it all away is strong, but I'm not that close to the end of my Ivydell rope yet.

"I just love all your stuff," she says. "Will you be selling from somewhere else after you leave here?"

"Most likely online. If you write your email address on that list there, I'll keep you updated."

"Oh, I'll definitely do that. Thanks."

More of Ivy's marketing genius. She says it'll all make sense to me once she gets my website set up.

"This is our first time here," the woman says as I put her stuff in a paper bag. "I've gotta say, your welcoming committee upfront is easy on the eyes."

"Stinger and Cujo do a good job at the gate."

"I'd be happy to open my gate for either one of them." She winks. "Maybe both if it was my lucky day."

A young girl nearby spins around with her eyes wide in horror. "Mom! Stop!"

She looks to be about thirteen, and she reminds me so damn much of Ivy's mom at that age. Cici was constantly telling Patty how embarrassing she was. I'd get so pissed off at that kid. And now I'd give anything to go back and take it all with a grain of salt, learn to laugh off the adolescent angst. I should've understood her better. This mom just rolls her eyes and smiles.

The mortified girl looks my way and cringes. "Sorry about my mother."

"Don't be. It's her job to embarrass you."

"She's an expert at it."

The mom shakes her head. "Okay, Shiloh. You've got to learn to lighten up, sweetheart. It was just a joke."

"Are you bored out of your wits today?" I ask the girl.

She sheepishly looks away. "I mean, this place is cool. It's just . . ."

"You probably have other people you'd rather be hanging out

with."

She smiles and nods. "I wish I could hang out with the cool woman I met earlier. She and her friends are probably having fun. No moms trying to embarrass them." Her pointed look at her mother is comical, but I manage not to laugh.

"Who'd you meet?" As if I have to ask.

"Her name is Ivy. Do you know her?"

"I do. I knew her mom when she was about your age. I knew her grandmother very well, too. And the younger guy at the gate with the scorpion tattoo on his neck is actually Ivy's boyfriend."

Shiloh looks at her mom with all the condescension she can muster. "Wow. I bet your feel dumb right now." She flounces off to go look at the soaps.

Her mom and I make eye contact. We both laugh.

"She'll outgrow it," I say.

"If I don't twist her head off first."

"Here. Have some lavender oil on the house. Rub it on your wrists, and take a whiff every time you feel the urge to do that."

"Thanks."

I watch the pair walk out together. Shiloh grabs onto her mother's arm excitedly. "Mom, it's a real live chipmunk! Look how cute!" All her surliness is gone in an instant.

"Let me try to get a picture of you with him in the background."

"Okay!"

They're out of my sight now, but I don't have to see Shiloh to know she's smiling. She'll be bored or embarrassed again soon, but right now, she's happy to be here.

Jensen

Brothers From Another Mother

THE CARS SLOW DOWN by mid-morning. Cujo and I keep stats on the out-of-state license plates to pass the time. So far, the farthest state we've seen is South Carolina. I think the most unlikely one we'll see is New York. He says Idaho. If either of those show up, the one who picked it owes the other one a steak. My bet for the one that we'll definitely see is Colorado. He says Arizona for sure. When the first one of those shows up, the one who didn't pick it owes the other one a six-pack of beer.

It's not like this is our first rodeo. We both know we haven't seen a plate from New York or Idaho come through the gate in the past, and we always see Colorado and Arizona. We've excluded Hawaii and Alaska, for obvious reasons.

So far, we've both been given notes from women with some form of contact information, email addresses, phone numbers, and social media accounts. Neither of us has any intention of reaching out to these women, so we're putting the notes all together and betting on how many we'll have by the time we close out the festival tomorrow evening. I say twenty. His optimistic ass says fifty. We haven't worked out the winner's prize for this yet.

Ivy sends me a pic of her and Josephine posing with Shadow at his forge. He's in his glory standing between the two of them.

> *Where's Zara?*

> *Dice stole her again!*

> *Should've known. Make sure Shadow's drinking water.*

> *We already made him take a hydration break. He bitched about it but he did it.*

> *If he's feeling good enough to bitch about something, he's feeling good enough.*

I show Cujo the picture.

"Jojo likes her a lot," he says.

"Ivy likes her, too. Does she factor into your future plans?"

"She has her own plans."

"Are you ever going to tell me what you're doing after Ivydell?"

"I haven't decided yet."

He's fucking with me, but he won't tell me his plans until he's ready.

"Arizona!" he yells.

I turn to watch the car approach. Damn. He won that one. "There's a six-pack in the shop fridge with your name on it."

"I thought we said twelve-pack?"

"No way. You've got to be sober enough to cook my steak."

"Shit, you'll be cooking me a steak as soon as that Idaho plate shows up."

I shake my head and laugh. After the car drives through, I hold up the business card the woman behind the wheel just slipped into my hand with an air kiss and a smile.

"How many is that?"

"Ten, I think."

"I thought it was twelve."

"You've got twelve on the brain."

A police car rounds the bend. We didn't make any bets about this. Texas plates, not that it matters.

The officer rolls down his window when he reaches the gate. "Who's in charge of this event?"

"Is there a problem?" I ask.

"Y'all have a permit?"

Aw, shit. Is he serious? This festival has been happening for decades.

"I'll text one of the owners. They're all working, so it may take a minute."

> Cop at the gate. He wants to see our permit.

> You've got to fucking be shitting me!

> Not really my style of humor. DPS. He's real.

> I'll be up there soon. Keep Cujo cool.

> It's all civil so far.

The cop pulls out of the way, parks, and gets out of his car. "Do y'all need some water?"

"No, we're good. But thanks."

He stares beyond us at the welcome sign.

"Feel free to walk in and read it," I say, hoping once he sees that this is a farewell festival, he'll leave us alone.

Cujo squares his shoulders as the officer walks past the gate. I try to see this through his eyes. He's not a huge fan of law enforcement. He doesn't say anything to the cop, but he looks at me and says, "We're not in any city limit."

"I'm not questioning a state trooper's jurisdiction. Petra's coming up. She'll handle the questions. We just live here, remember?"

He eyes me and nods. "I'm aware."

The officer comes back over and introduces himself. "This place is going away soon, huh?"

"It is indeed," I say. "Did you come out here because of one of the flyers?"

"Yeah, somebody saw one and called in, asking about it. I was in the area, so I said I'd come check it out. Lots of people from big cities moving into that new development. Everything around here is strange to them. And the locals think the new people are strange. Everybody's watching everybody since that cult compound got raided. You hear about that?"

"That was over an hour away from here, wasn't it? Don't see what that has to do with us. We're all adults. No kids live here."

"Eh, people get paranoid. Hell, I never even knew y'all were out here."

"How long you been a trooper?" I ask.

He laughs. "Fair question. Almost ten years, but I just started at this region. Nobody told me anything about this place, though, so I guess y'all must not cause much trouble."

"As far as I know, we ain't ever caused any trouble," Cujo says.

"I just need to confirm this is all kosher so we can tell the complainer that everything's in order. We don't want any civilians coming out here to raise hell."

"No, we don't want that at all," I say. "That's the last thing we need."

Cujo grunts. I think it was in approval with what I said.

The trooper walks back to his car and radios a message to someone, hopefully telling dispatch it's all good here. I can't make out what he's saying.

Another car arrives. We wave them forward. The driver stares suspiciously at the DPS car.

"Nothing to worry about," I say when the guy rolls down his window. New Mexico plates, so the smell of weed wafting from his vehicle is legal where he came from. Driving while smoking isn't, but there's no visible smoke and nobody is passing a joint or a vape pen around. Still, the scent alone could be construed as probable cause. We don't need civilians out here protesting, but we don't need anyone who comes in peace getting arrested at the gate either. "No fee this year. Sign ahead explains it all."

With a quick jerk of my head, I direct him to drive in.

He's halfway down the first dirt road by the time the trooper comes back to us. Thankfully, Petra drives up at the same time. She hops out of her car with paperwork in her hand.

I should've known she had something official. A sigh of relief escapes me. Cujo nods.

In less than thirty seconds, she's showing the officer her documents and they're shooting the shit like old friends. She has that way about her, honed from years of being the spokesperson for Ivydell—not to mention the numerous causes she's championed and disagreements she's mediated over the years. It's not the first time she's had to confront law enforcement or some asshat with an objection to something that didn't concern them to begin with.

She invites the trooper into Ivydell to look around the festival, but he declines, wishes us well, and turns his car around and leaves.

"You guys need anything up here?" she asks.

"That was it," I say.

"In all the years we've done this, no one has ever called the cops on us." She laughs. "It figures, doesn't it?"

"If that's the worst thing that happens, we'll be doing all right," Cujo says.

"It better be the worst thing that happens." She pats me on the shoulder and says, "Well, I've got to get back to selling the soaps your girlfriend packaged up all pretty for me."

"Thanks for making peace with that," I say.

"Not like there was a damn thing I could do to stop it," she says. "But I wouldn't have been me if I hadn't tried."

"Why though?"

She smiles, pulling creases at the corners of her eyes. "It had a lot less to do with you than you think."

That's enough of an answer for me. "Thanks."

"She's good for you."

"I'm going to be good for her, too."

"You don't have to prove anything to me, Stinger. You're good for each other. I see it."

She points at Cujo. "And as for you . . ."

He grumbles.

"Josephine's tough because she's had to be. Under all those tattoos and that hard stare is a tender young woman. I know she's independent, but don't you forget that she can still be hurt. Take care with her."

"What did I do wrong?"

"Nothing as far as I know, but as long as I've known you, I've never given you any advice. We don't have much time left together, and speaking up for her is worth pissing you off it that's what it does."

"I have no intentions of hurting Jojo."

"I didn't ask your intentions. I'm telling you to pay attention."

"Yes ma'am."

"Thank you. And for the record, I'd speak up for you, too, if I thought you needed it."

She throws us a wave out the window as she drives off.

"Shit," Cujo says. "I didn't think Mom was ever gonna leave."

I crack up. "Truth be told, we probably both could've benefitted from having a mom like her."

He watches her tires churn up dust. "Yeah. Crossing her path hasn't hurt me any."

Ivy

Women Helping Women

JOSEPHINE AND I WALK the rock-lined path all the way back to where it begins, which is near the Community Center. I'm surprised to find Tawny behind the counter. I was only hoping for some leftover baked goods. And I definitely assumed I'd have to make my own iced coffee. But no, Tawny has put away her easel and paintings, and opened a mid-day café.

"I don't know how you had time to get over here and bake cookies already, but thank you."

"I make big batches of cookie dough and freeze it. There's always cookie dough in the freezer here. Myrna adds to it occasionally, too."

"I cannot believe no one told me this!" I side-eye Josephine. "On second thought, it's probably a good thing I didn't know until my last week here."

There's a handful of festival people hanging out in the Community Center, drinking water or coffee and eating warm cookies, showing off their purchases to each other. I try to be casual about it, but I'm definitely checking to be sure none of them has bought Tawny's painting that I want. It wasn't with her in The Circle, and I haven't had a chance to stop by her and Leo's studio yet.

I don't see my painting, which is a relief. Hopefully, no one bought it and already drove away with it.

As we're leaving, Tawny says, "See you at The Circle later."

"At The Circle?"

"Well, yeah. Won't you be there tonight?"

"She will," Josephine says, pulling me toward the door.

"What's happening tonight?"

"The guys play and sing, and we all unwind. Usually, a handful of people who came for the festival linger and hang out with us. It's kind of a low-key party. Everyone's exhausted and they all have to get up and do it all over again tomorrow, but it's cool to hang out for a while."

"Those are my favorite times in Ivydell. I love wine night and community dinners. A low-key party in The Circle sounds great."

"You might not want to tell Stinger those are your favorite times."

"He knows how much I enjoy my time with him."

"I bet he does. Where did Zara and Dice go?"

"His place or hers, I guess."

"Talk about an instant attraction. But I'm not judging. For all we know, they're just playing poker." She shrugs and laughs.

"Yeah, strip poker, maybe." I shake my head. Zara and Dice's instalust was the last thing I expected to happen. "So, what's in the cards for you and Cujo?"

"We'll figure it out when the time comes."

"The time is coming pretty quick."

"Things work out however they're meant to."

"Have y'all not talked about it at all?"

"We have."

"You're not going to tell me."

"Not yet." Her smile is radiant. Whatever they've decided, she's happy about it. That's really all that matters. Of course, I still want the details, but for now, I'm good knowing that she's good.

"Are you going with Zara to her appointment with the Spirit Sisters at five?"

"I forgot about that. Yeah, I told her I'd go. You should come, too."

"I have to come. I have an appointment at the same time."

"Oh. Would you prefer I not be there?"

"No, I don't mind. They have separate session rooms in their work casita, anyway."

"I've never been in that casita. The one they live in freaks me out. I can't imagine how I'm going to react in their psychic offices."

Josephine laughs. "It's actually really calming."

"You've had a session with them before?"

"Two. They're good."

"I'll take your word for it."

"You should get a reading."

"I knew this was where you were headed. It's just not something I've ever been drawn to. Besides, I'm sure they're booked."

"Maybe. Maybe not. I'm ready for lunch, but I don't have any food at my place. I was supposed to go to the store yesterday, but when Cujo invited me to go fishing, that sounded like more fun. You want to leave for a while?"

"I have popcorn and peanut butter and jelly," I offer.

"Sold. Lunch at your place."

The road to our casitas is lined with parked cars. There is a truck blocking my driveway. "Good thing I didn't need to go anywhere."

"Someone should've told you if you think you might want to

leave, you need to move your own car to the road so you don't get blocked in."

"Someone, huh? Someone like my neighbor, maybe?"

"I assumed Petra probably told you everything you needed to know about the festival."

"I think she had other things on her mind. I guess everyone did."

"Yeah. It's weird. I think we're mostly all trying not to think about it."

"That's what I'm doing."

I make the popcorn the way I make it with Jensen, adding plenty of melted butter. Josephine makes our peanut butter and jelly sandwiches. I move the festival posters from my table to the counter, and it feels good to sit down in the relative silence I've gotten used to here.

For the first time, I pull the heavy curtains across my patio door. I don't want to have to worry about festival goers seeing us in here and thinking it's an open studio.

It's quieter in here than outside, but busy chatter and laughter still floats in. I like it, but don't at the same time. I've been looking forward to the festival, but it feels a little like an invasion of privacy.

Someone knocks on my door.

"Ignore it," Josephine says. "It's probably somebody wanting to use your bathroom instead of walking up to the Community Center."

"I have to answer it. It could be Zara."

It is Zara. She looks happy. Relaxed. No need to ask if she's been playing poker or having sex.

"Hungry?" I ask.

"Starving."

Josephine shoves the popcorn bowl over on the table so Zara can snack on that while I make her a sandwich. I make two more while I'm at it and cut them all in half. As soon as I set the plate of sandwiches on the table, someone else knocks on the door. This is a softer knock.

I pull the door open cautiously. It's Shiloh, the girl I met this morning.

"Hi," she says timidly. "I'm sorry to disturb you, but I saw your friend come in, and ummmm . . ." She shifts from one foot to the other.

She's clearly upset. "Come in. Are you okay?"

"Yeah." As soon as I've closed the door, sealing her safely inside with us, she says, "But I started my period. And I don't have anything with me, and if I tell my mom we have to leave to go to the store, she's going to be so mad at me. I've been kind of shitty to her a lot today."

"I'm sure she'd understand, but there's no need for you to leave. Bathroom. Under the sink. Help yourself."

"Thank you. I knew you'd help."

She looks at me like I've saved her life. I remember plenty of times when finding someone with an extra tampon felt like a life-saving moment, especially as a teenager.

"Women are supposed to help each other. You can pay it forward someday."

Her cheeks blush as she ducks her head and slips into my bathroom. Poor kid. I open my front door and look out to be sure her mom's not searching for her. I don't see her.

When Shiloh comes out of the bathroom, we give her some sandwiches wrapped in a paper towel. She looks around my casita so wistfully. I know she'd love to be invited to hang out with us, but her mom is going to be looking for her soon.

"Do you know where your mom is?"

"She's across the street, looking at some gross jewelry. God, I hope she doesn't buy one of those necklaces and wear it in front of my friends."

"Myrna's stuff isn't for everybody, that's for sure. But I'm glad you know where to find your mom."

"Yeah. Thanks again," she says.

"It happens to all of us at some point. I'm glad I could help."

"What do you do for your job?"

"Well, right now, I'm a graphic designer."

"Do you like it?"

"Mostly. But I might be about to make some changes."

"Because you can do that. You can just decide, and then make a change."

"Yep."

"Cool. Well, good luck with whatever you decide."

"Thanks. Good luck to you, too."

"Hey," Josephine says. "Did you get a poster?"

"No. Mom said we should wait until we were ready to leave so it wouldn't get bent, but now I think they're all gone."

"Well, here." Josephine grabs one from my counter. "I can sign it for you if you want."

"You're the artist?"

"I am."

"She's also a tattoo artist," Zara says.

"Whoa!" Shiloh's eyes light up.

"I cannot give you a tattoo. But I can sign a poster for you."

"Damn. But, yes to the signed poster. Please."

I toss a pen onto the table, and Josephine signs the poster for Shiloh.

She takes it gingerly like she's afraid to mess it up, careful not to let it touch the sandwiches in her other hand, and then she says goodbye to us and goes back outside.

"God, I wouldn't want to be that age again," Zara says.

"No way in hell." Josephine grabs a fistful of popcorn.

"Me either," I agree. "But if I could roll back time just a little, I'd take a do-over on a few things."

"Well, yeah," Zara says. "If we're wishing on stars."

"I have literally wished on stars in this casita." I stare at my bed.

"And I'm sure all your wishes came true," Josephine says, glancing at my bed with a smirk.

"Not yet. But they might."

We end up hanging out in my casita until it's time for their appointments with Alma and Elma. Neither of them knows which twin they're seeing. I wonder if some people have a preference.

The crowd has thinned tremendously by the time we walk out to head over to Whispering Winds B. "Wow. It feels almost deserted."

There are still several cars parked on the street, but so many have left. The festival turnout was mind-blowing, but it feels sad to see so few cars left.

"More people will come tomorrow," Josephine says. "I feel like maybe it's better for things to wrap up earlier this year. Almost like it makes the transition easier."

"I can see that. How long will the guys stay up at the gate?"

"They'll probably call it a day soon, if they haven't already."

Alma answers the door at unit B of their casitas. I'm not sure if I should step inside or wait out here, but she gestures for me to follow Zara and Josephine inside. There is a Victorian sofa for people who aren't getting a reading. I run my hand over the brocade fabric. "This is gorgeous."

"You'll find it comfortable, too," Alma says.

"Make yourself at home, dear." Elma fans her hand toward the kitchenette. "There is water in the kettle. Tea bags are in the canister."

"Do you want to come into the room with me?" Zara asks.

"No, that feels wrong. It's your personal information."

"Suit yourself, but I don't mind."

"I'll make some tea and wait out here."

Josephine has already followed Alma into one of the rooms. They're not proper rooms, not with doors or anything, but there are heavy beaded curtains hanging over the entrances. I brew a cup of tea and add honey and lemon. When they begin to speak, I can't make out words, just hushed voices.

Until Zara yells, "Hell, yeah!"

Elma's gentle laughter follows the outburst. At least she's getting good news.

I jump when I see the amethyst woman on the side table, thinking at first that she'd followed me. Which is ridiculous, of course, because the only way that could be the same figure from my casita is if I'd brought her with me. I turn her around to face the kitchen area, anyway.

The only light in the waiting area comes from a small beaded lamp. I can tell there are lamps in the reading rooms, too, but their glow doesn't brighten up anything out here. There are heavy curtains over the windows, and I'm sure they don't want me to open them and flood the space with sunlight.

So, I sit in the near dark and sip my tea, stealing looks at the amethyst woman to be sure she doesn't move. I know it's ridiculous, but it makes me feel better.

A painting on the wall next to the bathroom catches my attention. I recognize that stormy angel. It's Gran's work. Tears sting my eyes. Happy tears. She'd be so honored to know the Spirit Sisters still have one of her paintings hanging here.

I walk to the painting for a better look. It's not a watercolor. This is an oil painting, and as I stare at her fine brushstrokes, a movie plays in my mind. I see her standing in the same open area where I encountered the rattlesnake. Her hand moves so precisely, wind blowing through her hair, and prairie dogs playing a few feet away. She doesn't pay them any attention because she's too focused on her painting.

There are rain clouds hanging low in the sky. I can hear the thunder roll. She's young and beautiful, and so totally lost in her art. When I inhale, I can smell the rain washing the desert clean. It's all so real.

For the briefest moment, Gran and I are in Ivydell at the same time.

I can't touch her, and she can't see me, but I feel her with me.

On my next inhale, all I smell is my spearmint tea. The movie has ended. But the angel is still hovering on the canvas. My fingers trace her, and my eyes close as I map her from memory.

Josephine's laughter tumbles from the room closest to me. Nothing here is unsettling anymore.

The old sofa feels fancy, but familiar. I'd love to find one like this. It has so much more character with its curves than modern square furniture. Not that I can afford an antique like this, especially not if I might be about to implode my career. I sit back and imagine it's mine.

Its deep red fabric is framed by dark carved wood on the top and on the fronts of the arms. There is a heavy twisted fringe along the bottom. It's in pristine condition, and I am hopelessly in love with it.

I sit and stare at Gran's angel while I finish my tea.

Zara's session ends first. She comes out with a huge smile on her face.

Elma motions for me to come into the room.

"Oh, no," I say. "I'm fine."

"I paid for your session. You better go in there and use it." Zara doesn't wait for my response. She takes a cup and begins making herself some tea, as if this had been her plan all along.

Here goes nothing, I guess.

"You feel her, don't you?" Elma asks.

"I did for a moment."

"You will again."

Elma tells me my life is in flux, but good things are coming. Stability. Happiness. Pretty vague stuff, but it's nice to hear. Then, out of nowhere, she says that Mom is getting married soon. And Gran is thrilled about it.

Um, hello. Back the fuck up! My mother? Getting married? I don't see that happening. But it's better than being told something tragic is on the horizon. Although if Mom were here, I think she might disagree.

Elma stares at the space between us like she sees something there. All I see is the dark blue tablecloth beneath her clasped hands. She smiles and says, "Those little boys love their toy trucks."

"Yeah, it's crazy how instinctively some little boys just love trucks."

She stares at me. Oh, she wasn't speaking in generalities. What little boys? I could ask, I suppose. Nope. I stare back at her in silence.

"The little girl will love them, too." She chuckles. I have never heard either of these old women chuckle.

"She's going to give her big brothers a run for their money. She will be the more daring of the three."

She goes on as if she's in a trance. "Oh, how he is going to love teaching them about the grapes. Racing his own truck with theirs. He will become a big kid with them. You'll have to give some grace as he relives the things he missed out on, but he isn't immature, dear. Just fun-loving. And that can be a good thing."

Okay, this is starting to get uncomfortable. Is it hot in here?

Elma chuckles again.

I'm glad she's amusing herself. She said I could ask any questions. This seems like a good time to interject with one. "Will I regret leaving my job?"

"Oh, you will have so few regrets from here on out."

Well, that's good to know.

"A moment, please." Her eyes squint, and she tilts her head as if she's having trouble hearing something. "She says to tell you no stormy angels in the deciding room."

"The deciding room?"

"That's what I'm getting. Sometimes their messages don't come through in the same words we might've chosen. But they usually make sense in time."

I'd like it to make sense right now, thank you. What is a deciding room? A court room? A hospital room? I hate this message.

Again with the chuckling.

Come on, Gran. If you're really trying to tell me something, just say it.

"She says to relax, dear. Relax, Ivybug. That's what she says."

No one but Gran ever called me Ivybug. And she was the one who wanted me to be named Ivy Dell, but when she was being the kindest . . . when we were having the most fun together, I was Ivybug. Even after I was grown.

My eyes leak a little, and my chest constricts. Relax? Sure. I'll get right on that.

I don't believe in any of this. But, Ivybug? Shit. Three kids? A deciding room? My anxiety slips away, despite my best efforts to court worry. I want more answers. Want it all defined, but at the same time, I feel an underlying sense of serenity. None of this makes any sense.

Elma smiles softly, and says, "She's had to go, dear. But what lovely messages she brought."

Did she, though? Well, I'm not sleeping tonight.

I may never sleep again.

Jensen

Far-Flung Family

Cujo and I are drinking his six-pack prize when he gets a text from Josephine.

"Jojo says they're headed for The Circle. I guess we ought to make our way over there."

"Damn. Just like that, huh? She beckons, and you jump."

"Don't make me rearrange your pretty face."

I laugh as I stand and toss my empty can at the cardboard box I'm currently using for trash. "You got your guitar?"

"Jojo's grabbing it from my place on her way out there."

So many smartass responses run through my head, but I just smile. "All right. We walking?"

"You plan on drinking more?"

"I might."

"Then we're walking."

It's a clear night. Sky's full of stars, none of them falling as we walk the path.

A few strangers are seated on the wooden benches at The Circle. Most places, it would be concerning to have unknown people hanging around after dark. Any other time, I'd feel that way here, too. But things are different during the festival. Outsiders become a part of it all for a brief time.

Ivy's hair shines in the light of the waning gibbous moon. I envision her bare skin illuminated by the full moon in the bed of my truck, and I will my dick to stand down. Not that it does me any good.

Cujo walks to the front, and Josephine meets him with his guitar. Dice and Shadow are already tuning up. Cujo strums a few chords, and people stop talking to focus on the trio.

He doesn't have a mic, but with pipes like Cujo's, it's not needed. His bike is loud and abrasive. He is loud, too, but smooth.

The wide-open desert volleys his voice all the way to the mesa. I don't have to be out there to know. You can feel the momentum of it as it sweeps past you.

Ivy steps in front of me, and I wrap my arms around her to hold her against my chest. Her body sways and mine goes with her. If she needs to move, so do I.

Josephine and Zara wander over and stand on either side of us. These are my people, the ones standing with me, the musicians in front of us, and some of the amazing souls seated around us. They are from far-flung corners, but we're family. We will always know each other.

"You coming home with me tonight, beautiful?"

"You'll have to close the curtains on your patio door. I don't trust all these festival people to leave. I think some of them might just sleep on the ground or on the nearest patio."

"It has been known to happen." I squeeze her tighter. "But we will be hidden away from the world."

"Hidden away with you is my favorite place to be."

"Hmm, I don't think you mind being fully exposed on occasion."

She pinches my forearm. "Behave."

"For now."

"Exactly." Her head lolls back until her mouth reaches mine.

When we break the kiss, Zara and Josephine both rest their heads on my shoulders, essentially making me a leaning post for all three of these women.

Cujo looks out and smiles. Dice smiles, too. As much as Cujo strikes fear in the hearts of some, he's quicker to smile than they know. Especially for Jojo. Dice, however? That dude is stone when it comes to women. But right now, he's stone-cold smiling like a love-sick puppy.

I sneak a sideways glance at Zara's face and catch her smiling back at him. Looks like Ivydell is leaving no stone unturned on its way out.

Ivy
Private Reserve

PETRA PULLS A WAGON up next to us. There's a cooler in it, and when she flips the lid, I see it's filled with cans of beer and bottles of water. Zara passes Jensen a beer. He cracks it open right next to my ear, and the cool spritz that hits my cheek feels good.

Never imagined I'd enjoy having a mist of beer sprayed on my face, but it's not even enough to leave my skin damp. Just enough to remind me that this is all real.

When Cujo says this is the last song of the evening, some of the non-residents gather their things and head back to the path, using their phones to light the way. The last of them leave when the song is over.

"Today was fun," Zara says. "Let's do it again tomorrow."

She walks away, heading straight for Dice.

"See you in the morning," Josephine says.

"You sticking around for a while?" Jensen asks Petra.

"Yeah. Myrna and I are going to hang out and unwind for a bit longer. Y'all are welcome to join us, but I assume you have other plans." She scoffs and shakes her head like she's disgusted, but we both know she's just teasing us.

Myrna walks over, and she and Petra sit on one of the benches. Petra yawns and stretches her arms over her head and her legs out in front of her. Myrna sits cross-legged beside her with a fresh beer in her hand.

Before I came to Ivydell, the thought of two women sitting alone at night in the middle of the desert would've scared the hell out of me. Now, I just say goodnight.

Their laughter trails us as we walk away.

Jensen pulls the curtains across his patio doors like we talked about earlier, but I'm pretty sure the only people left in Ivydell tonight are residents. I don't tell him to reopen them, though. There is an added level of sensuality to being truly hidden here with him.

"I could use a shower."

"We could both use a shower," he says. "But you can go first."

I'm grateful he didn't push the option of showering together. As much as I want us to be together right now, I really just need an unbothered, hot cleansing shower.

The smell of popcorn greets me when I step out of the shower, and it makes me smile. This smell is so coded for me now. It's him. Us. Bliss.

I towel-dry my hair, wrap the towel around my body, and walk out of the bathroom. Jensen is leaning against his kitchen counter, eating popcorn, looking exhausted.

"Did you eat dinner tonight?" I ask.

"I drank dinner tonight."

"Do you want me to make you something more substantial than popcorn?"

"All I have is—"

"Eggs and cheese." I finish the sentence for him because I already know. "When I met you, you kept a lot more food in your fridge."

"That's because I didn't have you taking up all my free time yet. I still had time to go to grocery store back then."

"Right. You still find time to buy wine."

"You like wine. I buy it for you."

"Sure. Do you have bread?"

"Yeah."

"How about I make us grilled cheese sandwiches while you're in the shower?"

"If you're offering, I'm eating."

My eyes flit involuntarily to the popcorn bowl. He laughs and grabs a handful of popcorn to eat on his way to the bathroom.

His eyes roll back in his head when he takes the first bite of his grilled cheese. "It tastes so good because you were naked when you cooked it."

"I was wearing a towel."

"Shh. Don't ruin my dinner."

I toss a piece of popcorn at his face. He catches it in his mouth. "I was trying to hit you, not feed you."

"Why would you want to hit me after I paid you a compliment?"

"I'm just mean like that."

"Yeah, I forget what a monster you are sometimes."

He pops the last bite of his grilled cheese into his mouth, and I hand him what's left of mine. I don't have to twist his arm. It's gone in two bites.

"Come sit with me." He stands and takes my hand.

With his back pressed to the headboard, he spread his legs, causing the towel around his waist to come untucked. I drop mine to the floor and sit between his legs. His warm hands rub down my arms while my back rests against his chest.

"Are you ready to leave this place behind?" I ask.

"Yes."

I'm shocked at how quickly he answers, how resolute he sounds about it.

"But you'll miss it."

"Mostly, I think I'll just be thankful for the memories. And for the healing. I'm leaving here a much stronger man than when I showed up."

"Being here has changed me, too. I don't mean to compare it to what you experienced. I'd never make light of what you went through. And I know I've hardly been here any time at all, but I feel like a whole different person."

"You don't have to explain yourself to me. The depth of my changes doesn't invalidate yours. You were in pain when you got here."

"More than I knew."

"I think I might've loved you the moment I recognized the hurt in your eyes. All I know is that I do now. I love you, Ivy."

"I love you, too."

"My mind is spinning all these big plans for the future, and you're in all of them. I don't want to put any pressure on you, but I need you to know that you feel permanent to me. I know this was only meant to be a temporary escape for you, but where are you at on leaving here with something permanent as a possibility?"

"I'm honestly in a place where I believe anything's possible. A place where I believe in all sorts of magic, even romance." I sigh dramatically, and he wraps his arms around me.

"Of all the things I thought I might find in the desert, I couldn't have fathomed you."

"It's strange to think how easily we could've missed ever meeting each other. If I'd waited a few more months to reach out to Petra, Ivydell would've been gone. You'd have been out there falling in love with someone else."

"No. Every other woman who entered my life would've been temporary. Until I met you out there in some other place, because I think we would've eventually met somehow."

"Maybe I'd have stumbled into your winery, tipsy and giggling in my heels with a bachelorette party. But you'd have taken one look at me, rolled your eyes, and avoided me at all costs."

"Not even. I'd have taken one look into your eyes, seen my future, and held you captive in the barrel room until you fell in love with me."

"Damn. Remind me to check the barrel room at Vintage Vibes for hostages on a regular basis."

He laughs. "You better not let me catch you alone in there."

"Oh, yeah? You think you'd be compelled to take advantage of me between the racks?"

His hand glides up my ribcage until it's between my breasts. He slides it up and down. "I'm thinking about putting something between this rack right now."

"Are all vintners horny teenage boys at heart?"

"Well, probably not the ones who are women."

"Cool. Thanks for clearing that up."

I turn around and straddle him. "Your winery is going to be a raging success, Jensen. And you're going to deserve every bit of it. Don't ever doubt that."

"I hope so, because I am finally ready for that stage of my life."

"I'm envious. I wish I knew what came next for me professionally."

"How would you feel about running a tasting room at a fledg-ling biodynamic winery?"

"I'm not a sommelier."

"You don't need a license. You just need the knowledge. If you're interested, I could teach you everything you'd need to know. You'd be there from the beginning, so you'd know all there was to know about our wines."

Our wines?

"I'm not sure I could afford to make that kind of career change right now."

"I can pay you whatever you need to make, Ivy."

"I don't want you paying my bills, Jensen."

"I'd be paying you a salary, just like anyone else would. I'm not trying to buy anything beyond that. I know I'm asking you to make a big move in more ways than one. I also know how independent you are. I'd like you to move in with me, too, but I understand if you'd rather have your own place."

"Until the winery is up and running, there wouldn't be anything for me to do."

"You have no idea how much work there is to be done between now and then. Wouldn't you rather be involved in all the early decisions? I'm going to need a marketing manager and an event planner, too."

"Oh, now the truth comes out. You expect me to do the job of three people."

"We'd run the tasting room together. I can manage the vine-yards, and you can handle the administrative stuff. As we grow, you can decide when you're ready to give up any portion of your job, and we'll hire someone specifically for that. Someone we both agree is a good fit."

"I had no idea you wanted to include me on a such a grand scale. I mean, this is your *dream*."

"You're right. Shit, I'm sorry. I didn't mean to make assumptions. I just would really love to have you be an integral part of it, but I see it now. It's not fair to ask you to give up your own dreams to support mine."

"No, that's not what I meant at all. I don't have a dream job or business plan, Jensen. I'm honestly flattered, just a little overwhelmed. This isn't something I ever considered. It's an amazing offer, but what if I'm all wrong for it?"

"I have a pretty good idea what kind of people work well in the wine business. You're creative and passionate. You care about people, and you know how to make them feel welcome. And you like wine."

"You really think that's enough, huh?"

"I know it is."

"When it comes to my work, I like a lot of creative control."

"Take on as much as you want."

"I'm going to want to design the logo and all the signage."

"Feel free."

"The décor, too."

"Go for it."

"Your dick is pretty hard right now. Are you sure that's not driving all this agreeability? What if there's not enough blood left in your brain to be thinking clearly?"

"I promise to remain agreeable to all these terms even without a hard-on. You can test me later."

"I get to name all the wines, too."

"Hmmm, I'll take your opinion on the wine names into consideration. That's the best I can offer on that one."

"I'm going to have to learn all that pretentious wine-speak, aren't I?"

"That plus all the pompous biodynamic bullshit on top of it."

"Oh, no. We're going to be insufferable wine people. All earthy and organic and obnoxious. It's going to become our whole personalities."

"It's already in your blood. I can feel it."

"Oh, yeah? Is that what you feel?" I rock my pussy along the thick vein running up the underside of his cock.

"Feels like a good year." He flips our bodies. "But it's impossible to be sure until I've tasted it."

"Just so we're clear, this isn't what you had in mind when you said you wanted me to make people feel welcome in the tasting room, right?"

His sexy grin makes me feel like I have champagne bubbling in my veins.

"No, Ivy Dell McAdams. This is my private reserve." His tongue swipes through my seam, and an effervescent fizz flows throughout my entire body. "It doesn't get poured for anyone else."

"It's just Ivy."

"Just mine." His body flattens against the mattress, and he buries his face in his private reserve.

I think I'm going to like having a workplace romance.

Josephine
In The Wind

I watch Cujo sleeping next to me in my bed. His rattlesnake is healing remarkably well for someone who refuses to follow aftercare instructions.

Of all the ways I've shocked my family, they aren't ready for him. I smile, knowing I wasn't ready for him either. And also, I don't give a shit what they think. Not anymore. I get it now: you can love people without needing their approval, but sometimes, that requires loving them from a distance. Maybe we can bridge the gap someday.

The wind's blowing like a motherfucker tonight. It rattles my front door with every gust. When I first came here, that noise would wake me from a sound sleep. I'd bolt upright, convinced someone was trying to break into my casita. Even in Ivydell, I lock my doors before I go to bed.

But no one was ever coming for me, not to hurt me or to save me. It was always just the wind, the same wind that's blown me between here and Albuquerque and back again. I'll be riding it between Albuquerque and Vegas with the same frequency soon, but in a plane instead of a car.

Me, a frequent flyer. Never saw that coming, but here it comes. I'm not afraid. I'm ready for a more hectic schedule, and I know how to recognize the signs if I need a break. And the big bear of a guy sleeping next to me will see them if I don't.

I took care of myself for so long, however haphazardly, that I didn't even know how to let someone else in. But he didn't wait for an invitation either. He just crashed into my life and claimed me. I could kick him out any time, but I think we both know I'm not going to at this point.

No matter how often I feel the need to remind him that he doesn't own me, he never gets mad. He just nods along and reassures me he's not trying to own me. He's just trying to love me. I put up a hell of a fight, but his big stubborn ass wouldn't give up on me.

How do you not fall stupidly in love with someone who sees all your complicated messed-up shit and calls it beautiful? When you show them your worst, and they wait for you to get it out of your system because they saw right through you all along. When they say you make them better, and you can't imagine how because they've always seemed too good to be true to you.

But they keeping being good. Until one day, you stop trying so hard to find a reason. You just breathe. And believe.

Jensen

Day Two Dawns

It's still dark out, but there is a faint light coming in around the curtains. It's day two of the festival. This is the end. Ivy rolls over next to me without waking.

And there's my new beginning.

She'd tell me not to think things like that. She'd say I could accomplish all my goals whether she was around or not, and she'd be right. But they wouldn't mean as much without her there to share them.

I don't need anyone to tell me life doesn't come with a guarantee. We might not work out. Anything could happen, but I know now that even if love fades or ends in tragedy, it's still worth it. Because that feeling when you have it? It's everything.

You can live without it, but eventually, the memory of having it is probably going to make you want to try again.

Ivy opens her eyes. "If waking up with you staring at me is going to be a regular occurrence, I definitely cannot live with you."

"I'd still watch you sleep, whether we lived together or not."

"Noooo, don't say creepy things like that."

"I can't help it. It's fascinating the way you can drool that much and not wake up."

"I was not drooling in my sleep." She wipes the corner of her mouth just to be sure. "How much time do you have before you have to be at the gate?"

I fold the covers back to expose my morning wood. "How much time do you need?"

"Let's find out." Her sleepy smile and messy hair are gorgeous. She slides down my side and crawls between my legs. When she looks up at me as she licks my dick from the base to the tip, I see the playful teasing side of her that I love, but I also see a woman I'm ready to drop all my defenses for.

We never closed the gate last night, and we're not charging an entry fee, so maybe I don't need to rush out there. "Take your time, beautiful."

She closes her perfect mouth over the head of my dick, and my eyes shut. There are no words to describe how amazing it feels when her warm wet mouth slides down, taking as much as she can before she moves back up. I resist the desire to sink my fingers into her hair and guide her because I don't want to rush this. However she wants to do it, I'm just going to lie here and enjoy it.

When she hollows her cheeks and bobs her head faster, my hips lift up to meet her, to thrust deeper. Her soft fingers cradle and squeeze my balls, and I feel my dick touch the back of her throat in the same moment.

I can't keep my hands to myself any longer.

Pressing at the back of her head, I urge her to take more. She gags and pauses to take a breath. Her eyes are teary, but her mouth sinks lower, taking nearly all of me now. Her tongue moves against the underside of my cock, and it lurches in her mouth, tripping her gag reflex again. I'm going to come if she keeps doing that. Fuck, I'm close.

She pulls off completely, and I groan in protest, but when she climbs on top of me and replaces her mouth with her hot, wet pussy, I open my eyes and smile. Her hair falls over her tits, just long enough for the ends to brush across her nipples when she rocks up and back.

So fucking sexy. She rides my dick until we're both panting. "Don't stop," I beg when she slows down.

Shaking her hair off her chest, she rolls her head back until it falls behind her shoulders to fully expose her breasts. She palms them, pinches her nipples and pulls. It gets me closer, but I'm not there yet.

"Ride me harder, baby."

Her hands leave her tits. She splays them on my chest and plants her feet flat on the mattress with her toes turned out and her knees pointed at the ceiling, spreading her legs as wide as they can go in this position, giving me a clear view of her pussy pumping my cock. Yesss, this is exactly what I want.

"Damn that juicy little snatch looks so good stretched around my cock."

Her tits bounce and my balls tighten. My dick jerks, and I'm there. She doesn't stop until I'm fully spent.

She rolls off me and onto her back. I roll onto my side and kiss her shoulder. "Do you want a towel or an orgasm?"

"Both. Reverse the order, though."

"Damn, you're bossy."

"Don't act like we haven't met."

I kiss her shoulder again, and then I cup her pussy, letting my thumb circle her swollen clit. She moans, and I know I've found the right pressure and pace. Her hips buck gently, and I slip two fingers into her pussy. When her hips rock harder, I suck her nipple and finger her faster, trying to keep the momentum of my thumb steady as it works her clit.

Her shoulders tense and her thighs shake for a few seconds before her breathing shallows. And then it shortens to the clipped shrieks that just might be my favorite sound in the whole damn world. Feeling her fall apart under my hand and my mouth is so fucking hot. I plant kisses around her nipple after I release it.

Pulling her into my chest, I make sure to keep my eyes open because if I close them again, I'll be back asleep in a matter of seconds. She snuggles against me, all warmth and softness. Yeah, I've got to get out this bed. I kiss the top of her head before I pull away and slide my legs over the edge.

"I'm going back to sleep," she mumbles.

I stand, and my tired muscles waver. "Damn. You stole all my strength."

"Really? You're going to whine like that after I did all the work?"

She throws a pillow at my back, and I laugh, knowing she's always going to challenge me. And I'm always going to love it. I toss the pillow back at her and walk to the bathroom, wishing that I could get back in my bed instead.

I'm splashing water on my face when I think I hear voices. I turn off the water and confirm that Ivy is talking to someone at the door. The door closes, and I peak out of the bathroom. "Who was that?"

"Myrna. She brought us coffee and Tawny's homemade cinnamon rolls. Said she wanted to make sure we got some before they were gone."

"She's always been my favorite."

"I'm telling Petra you said that."

"She'll know it was just the cinnamon roll talking." I take a warm gooey bite and smile.

"You are definitely her golden boy."

"Why do you say that?"

"Are you serious? Petra adores you. I think she was afraid I was going to break your heart."

"No, I'm pretty sure she was afraid I was going to break yours."

"If things work out between us, she'll probably take credit for it. Tell everybody she introduced us."

"And we'll let her."

"Yep," she says with icing in the corner of her mouth. "But we'll both know you threw yourself at me."

"Huh, I distinctly remember you literally throwing yourself at me in front of your casita."

"I don't remember you pushing me away." The tip of her tongue clears the icing.

"Never." I kiss her sweet lips, and then force myself to get dressed.

Myrna

Let Them

I AM ENTIRELY TOO damn old to stay up as late as I did last night. It's not like I was out dancing until the wee hours, but I may as well have been. Hell, I don't even know how long Petra and I sat out there on that bench talking, but I know we both needed it. I'm whipped, though. No regrets, just consequences. Surely, this third cup of coffee will kick in any minute now.

The sun will be up soon, and the festival will be in full swing shortly after. Full swing looks different this year, but I sold a lot of jewelry yesterday. Maybe letting everyone know this is the last festival encouraged them to buy more. They seemed to make quicker decisions, too, not so much circling back to decide the way they usually do.

Impulse buys don't hurt my feelings any. If I'm lucky, the trend will continue today.

Ivy sure looked happy to see those cinnamon rolls when she opened Jensen's door. But young people in love always look happy. I wish the best for those kids. Petra is still worried about both of them, but that's her way. When she cares, she worries.

She's the best friend I've ever known, and the one I'll worry about the most as we all leave this place behind. She's a survivor. We both are. There are worse labels to wear, but it'll make your heart a little hard sometimes.

Petra's has softened in recent years. I hope the world doesn't take that from her again.

I'm ready to get back out there, find some new inspiration, refill my well. So many good things have happened for me because I ventured out and put my feet on foreign soil. It's time to set sail again.

No homebase this time. Not for a while, anyway. Just a vagabond with a keen eye for opportunity, a kick-ass pair of shoes for every occasion, a good red lipstick, and a mouth bold enough to wear it.

If that's all anyone recalls about me after I'm gone, I'll be well-remembered.

Of course, some people will always be hung up on the fucking bear. But that's none of my business. Let them fret. I've got places to be.

Signs Everywhere

I STAND IN FRONT of the Community Center and watch cars drive in for day two of the festival while I drink my coffee. Zara waves as she walks down the dirt road toward me, no different from the way she waves if we see each other on the beach or in town, her arm stretched high and moving side-to-side. She doesn't do anything on a small scale, not even waving. I wave back, even though she'll be standing in front of me in less than a minute.

Being here has felt natural from the very beginning, but I thought that was because I had a connection to this place through Gran and Mom. Yet, here's Zara, waving like seeing me here is no different from running into me at the beach.

"Where's Josephine?" she asks.

I shrug. "Haven't seen her yet. Cujo's at the gate. Maybe she went back to sleep after he left. She has trouble sleeping sometimes. I'll give her a little while before I go wake her up. How's Dice?"

"He was fine when he left last night."

"He didn't stay with you?"

"No. I didn't feel like having overnight company."

"So, you just told him to leave?"

"I didn't have to. He's pretty good at picking up on a vibe. Did you know his real name is Danté? Why go by Dice when you have a cool name like that?"

"I had no idea." It is a pretty great name, but I can't see him as anything other than Dice. That's his name to me. "I wonder what Cujo's real name is?"

"I hope it's actually Cujo because Cujo and Jojo is the cutest couple-name ever."

"Yeah, but I wouldn't tell him that."

"He knows it's cute when he calls her Jojo," she says. "You can tell by the way his voice changes when he says it. And his eyes light up."

"They do, don't they? I think there's more to their relationship than either one of them wants to admit."

"Same. Speaking of relationships, you plan on moving Stinger to the beach?"

"No. He's got his winery and vineyard plans. He'll be closer, but not at the beach."

"Where will you be?"

I'm not ready to talk about that yet. I'm not even ready to make a final decision about that yet. "I'll be at the beach. For a while, anyway. I've still got almost six months left on my lease."

"What are those people doing over there?"

I look toward the gate and see two SUVs pulled off the road. Both have the liftgates raised, and someone is passing out signs. "Oh, shit. It looks like we've got ourselves a protest."

"Cujo's watching them, too."

There is a line of cars still driving in, and Jensen is talking to each driver, but I can tell he sees what's happening. I text Petra.

Two women walk closer to the gate with their signs held high.

As Zara and I walk toward the gate, these sign-carrying people stretch across the road to block traffic. They're preventing more cars from coming in.

Jensen turns and shakes his head, throwing his arms up in the air.

"Petra's on her way," I say.

"Thanks."

"What devilish things do they think are going on at this festival?" Zara asks. "Why would anyone block people from coming in to look at art and walk around in nature?"

Cujo looks like a bull ready to charge. He paces back and forth inside the gate a few times before he stops to watch Petra's tires churning up dirt as she barrels toward us. "She's got Myrna with her!" he yells.

I look to be sure I heard him right. "Oh, shit. She'll eat these wingnuts for breakfast."

"Yeah," Zara says. "She's little, but you can just tell she's got some fire."

"Oh, she's got some fire all right," Jensen says. He walks to meet them when they get out of the car.

We all huddle together as the protestors begin to chant, "Jesus hates hippies and perverts! Jesus hates hippies and perverts!"

"I called that trooper that came out yesterday," Petra says, pinching the bridge of her nose. "Let's all just stand back until the cops can move these people out of the way. It makes no sense. With all the injustice in the world, our festival is what these people feel the need to make signs about?"

"You know it's not just the festival," Myrna says. "Those people are ruled by fear, and they've been taught to fear anything they don't understand. Hell, their own curiosity must terrify the shit out of them."

Zara nods. "It's easier for some people to be told what to think."

"Who would choose that?" I ask.

Petra shakes her head at the protestors, still chanting in the road. "Some people get beaten down by the world, and they just need life to be easier in some way. Making your own decisions is harder than letting someone else decide for you. And then there are the unfortunate ones who are born into that way of life and don't get to choose for themselves, at least not for a long time."

"No way," I say. "How could that ever be easier? Letting someone else make my decisions would be so much harder for me."

"That's because you weren't raised in fear. You were raised by strong women who taught you to think for yourself, to know that if you choose wrong, you can face it and make another choice. The opposite of following is leading, but sometimes, you only need to lead yourself. You're not a follower, Ivy. Those people are followers who don't know how to lead themselves. Whether it's by choice or because it's all they've ever known, they're followers."

She's right. I was born to a teenage mother, and still I wasn't born into fear. Yet here I am, dreading the personal decisions that lie ahead for me instead of embracing them. If I choose wrong, I can choose again. But the choices are mine to make.

Josephine's tires slide in the dirt as she slams on her brakes. She bounces out of her car like she's on a spring. "What's going on?"

"Just a bunch of damn idiots with too much time on their hands," Cujo says.

She goes to stand next to him. One of the protestors turns to see what we're doing and takes notice of Josephine. "Tattooed Jezebels will burn in the infernal flames of hell!"

That's it. Cujo charges. He yanks the guy's sign from his hand and tosses it out into the desert, and then he lifts the guy off his feet and tosses him in the same direction. To his credit, he throws the guy with a lot less force than he did the sign. He's not doing his worst; he's just making a point.

"Goddammit, Cujo!" Petra yells. "Do not put your hands on these people!"

"He fell." He glances over his shoulder at the stunned man who fell out of his hands moments ago. "Right after he dropped his sign. Clumsy fucker, I guess."

The guy gets to his feet and stumbles back toward the road.

Cujo squares his shoulders and yells, "Go pick that sign up! You can't just come out here and throw your shit around!"

For a second, I think the guy might actually be stupid enough to challenge Cujo, but then he turns and walks out through the scrub to get his sign.

The cars at the front of the line begin to honk, drowning out the chants. Cars behind them join in until a chorus of honking sounds off continuously. Some people turn up their music, others hang out the windows of their cars and yell obscenities at the protestors.

This could get out of hand quickly. And for what?

Myrna is practically vibrating with rage next to me. "There's eight of them and seven of us," she says. "That's a fair fight. And I've got my stomping boots on. I'm ready."

Cujo looks down at his own boots and then back up at Myrna. He raises his eyebrows and smiles. "Me, too."

"No!" Petra and Jensen yell in unison.

I check out Myrna's *stomping boots.* They're turquoise-dyed leather with embossed flowers all over them. I doubt the person who hand-tooled that design intended the wearer to use them to stomp anyone, but they do look like they could get the job done. Though they'd probably be more effective in a larger size.

Red and blue lights strobe. The line of cars waiting to enter the festival moves to the side, making room for the cops to proceed.

Within ten minutes, they have the protesters climbing back into their vehicles. The trooper from yesterday comes over to talk to Petra.

"How do you suppose we got on their radar?" she asks.

"I'm pretty sure they're members of that cult that got raided recently. One of them said something about it being hypocritical that some groups get targeted while other are free to fornicate and do witchcraft. We've advised them this is private property and not to come back, but you might want to keep an eye out."

"We've posted flyers for the festival every damn year," Myrna says. "And suddenly, on our last year here, they attract all the wrong attention. Why is that?"

"Ma'am," the officer says in a defeated tone, "We live in a society full of people who've lost their critical thinking skills. I think some of them don't even want to think for themselves anymore."

"Those people have always been around," Petra says. "Maybe they're too lazy to think for themselves, or maybe they're just too damn scared. Sometimes, they're dangerous, but mostly, they're just harmless idiots who've been brainwashed. The problem is you can't always tell the difference."

"Between me and you," the trooper says, "I think these are the harmless variety."

"Let's hope so," Jensen says. "And let's get these cars moving again so our unwelcome guests can turn around get the hell out of here."

"We'll stick around until they're off your property. Can't guarantee they won't hang around to carry their signs at the freeway, but we've told them they can't block your road."

"We can take it from here," Cujo says.

Petra gives him a stern look.

"Yeah, we've got it," Myrna says.

Petra gives her double the look.

Jensen waves more cars through the gate. The honking starts up again, and people cheer. We've got plenty of support. The protestors are outnumbered by dozens of carloads of people who are happy to be here.

"Come on," I say to Myrna. "We'll walk you back to your studio."

Petra gives me a grateful smile and mouths, *thank you*.

Myrna pats Cujo on his forearm. Her small hand looks like a child's against his muscles. "If they come back, you call me."

"I'll catch up in a little while," Josephine says.

She and Petra stay at the gate while Zara and I walk Myrna away from it.

Zara says, "I need to look through your pendants again. I still haven't decided which one I want to buy."

I rub the silver sparrow resting on my chest and slide it on its chain, hoping Zara chooses something from this collection, but knowing there is no telling what she'll take home from Ivydell.

Dice slows his car to a stop next to us. "Is everything okay up here?"

"Yeah," Myrna says. "It's all taken care of."

Shadow holds up a blacksmith hammer from the passenger seat. His long white hair is windblown, making him look like a madman. "We'll go make sure."

"Don't let Petra see that," Myrna says.

He lowers his hammer, and Dice drives on, but not before giving Zara a look. It's the kind of look that has a clear meaning between two people, but leaves everyone around them wondering.

"What the hell does that old man think he's going to do with that hammer?" Zara says.

"Whatever he decides needs doing," Myrna says. "It's his hammer."

She is the tiny, walking epitome of no fucks to give. And I think that may be exactly why I like her so much.

Zara bursts into laughter. "Okay then. His hammer, his choice."

We all laugh, but between Jensen and Dice, Shadow won't get to swing his hammer at any protestors. Cujo would probably hold him back, too. I think.

Tawny comes running up behind us from the Community Center. "Do I need to get Leo up here?"

"No," I turn and yell. "They've got it under control."

"Okay," she stops and yells back, "You gals stay safe!"

"We're good. I'm stopping by your studio later."

"I'll be there this afternoon. Come see me in The Circle this morning." She waves, and then I watch her pull out her phone. She's probably calling Leo, anyway.

"I wonder why Alma and Elma didn't see those people coming." I say.

Myrna shrugs. "Who's to say they didn't? They don't have to tell us everything they know. Maybe they hold back information sometimes, if they think it's for the best."

"I bet they do," Zara says.

Well, damn. That had never occurred to me. What if they know stuff about me that they haven't shared? Not that I'm necessarily convinced they know anything about anyone's future. But Elma did call me Ivybug. That didn't come out of thin air.

A car honks behind us, so we move over. They had plenty of room to go around us, but whatever. The passenger's window is down. "Excuse me," she says when they pull alongside us. "Do y'all know if an artist named Patrice McAdams is here this year?"

My heart thunders in my chest. Myrna takes my hand in hers.

"No," she tells them. "She's been gone from Ivydell for years."

"Damn," the woman says. "Do you know how we could get in

touch with her?"

"I'm her granddaughter," I say. Her face brightens. "But she died nearly eight months ago."

"Pull the car over!" The man driving stops at the edge of the road, and the young woman hops out. She runs back and throws her arms around me. "I have to give it to you then. Pop the trunk!"

We watch as she pulls a blanket from the trunk. She begins to unwrap whatever is inside. I can tell right away it's a canvas. "She painted this in Las Vegas."

The only time I'm aware of Gran being in Las Vegas was when she and Petra went to confront the man who got Mom pregnant with me. Although, now that I think about it, she probably went to help Mom get settled into college there—not knowing she'd be back so soon to move her home again. How'd she find the time to paint anything while she was there for any of those situations?

"I never knew she created any paintings in Las Vegas."

"My grandmother lived there. They were friends. Both artists. I don't how much painting Patrice McAdams did in Nevada, but she painted this. It hung in my grandmother's house for as long as I can remember. She raised me, so I grew up with this painting. Before my grandmother died, she made me promise I would return it to Patrice or her family. Said she knew it wasn't my style, but she didn't want it donated to a thrift shop or discarded."

I brace myself as she begins to turn the canvas to show us the painting. What kind of angels did Gran paint in Nevada?

It's a stretch of desert seen through a car windshield in the rain. Some of the raindrops are exaggeratedly large, and there are images inside them, all watery and wavy. There's the welcome to Vegas sign in one. In another drop, I find the backside of the sign, the one you see when you're leaving. There's a neon sign that says MAGIC but the letter I is burned out and broken with the bottom of a bullet visible between the halves as if it's been shot through. I don't need the Spirit Sisters to interpret that symbolism.

Everything is so distorted, but intricately detailed.

Searching the rest of the drops, I recognize an upside-down dragonfly. There is a small spilled bottle in one—dark glass, no label, but it's definitely not meant to be liquor. Medicine, maybe. Poison? There's a small bird in one. Even through the distortion, it's distinctly a sparrow.

The hair on the back of my neck stands up. "What's your name?"

"Glynnis."

"I'm Ivy. This means more to me than you could ever know. I'm so grateful your grandmother kept it. Thank you for coming here, for trying to find Gran to return it to her. I truly don't have words to explain what I'm feeling right now."

"I can't believe I just found you walking along the road like this. It's like fate."

"Did you ever meet my grandmother?"

"No, but I've seen pictures. She apparently stayed with my grandmother a few times when she came to Vegas, but I don't remember her ever visiting while I was growing up."

"Do you have pictures of our grandmothers together?"

"Probably. Give me your email address, and if I come across any, I'll send them to you."

We exchange email addresses and hugs, and then she hops back into the car. They drive away to find a place to park. I hope they have a great time here today.

Josephine and Myrna stare at me with their eyes wide and their mouths hanging open.

"What?"

Zara blinks. "You don't even seem fazed. Did that feel normal to you?"

"A lot of extraordinary things have happened to me here."

Myrna shakes her head. "She's not as uptight as she looks."

"No, she's really not."

"Y'all can quit talking about me like I'm not standing right here."

Myrna opens her studio while Zara and I drop Gran's amazing painting off at Sparrow's Song.

While we head across the street so Zara can buy herself a piece of Wild Love, Wizard prances in front of us as if we need a guide. We let him lead the way, but he doesn't take us to the door. He splits off at the edge of Myrna's yard and never once looks back to see if we're following.

Shadow

It'll Do

I MIGHT NOT BE the biggest fan of this festival, but I ain't letting no outsiders ruin the last one. Dice parks by the gate, and we get out to talk to Stinger and Cujo.

"What do you plan on doing with that hammer?" Stinger asks.

"Whatever needs doing."

Dice sighs. "I told him to leave it in the car."

"I've had this hammer for over sixty years. I'll take it wherever I damn well please."

Cujo nods. "Sounds fair to me."

These boys might need backup, and I'm not as much help as I once was, but I can still swing this hammer, so I keep it with me at the gate.

A warm breeze blows through my hair. I've still got plenty of it, but this desert has seen it go from dark to white, along with my beard. I've changed a lot more than this land has over the years. Within months of us clearing out, it'll be a completely different place. There won't be nothing left out here for us anymore, no reason to come back.

No more Ivydell.

Windmills.

Hell, truth be told, I'm not against progress, and I don't begrudge the women for selling. That's just life. But I got a little more processing to do before I can fully accept it. I bet we all do.

I look at these young men with so much life ahead of them, and part of me thinks it's good they're being forced away from here and back out into the world. I've got people who think I should've tried harder to fit in and build a life, get married, start a family, all that traditional shit. They all said I'd regret it one day.

They were all wrong because I don't do regret, but I'm still glad to see these guys moving on.

The world's different now. There's less of us hideaway types left, I guess. Dice says I'm a dying breed. I told that gambling son-of-a-bitch that I ain't dying yet. He just laughed. We both know I knew what he meant.

I'll die someday, same as anybody else, but I don't sense it coming for me too soon. Until then, I guess I'll go live with my niece and her husband in Arizona. They got some land, and they already built me a little cabin on it. It ain't my desert, but it'll do.

It's enough space to pick my guitar and swing my hammer.

It'll do.

Jensen

Matters of Perspective

ONCE THE PROTESTERS MOVE out, the procession of festival attendees goes smoothly. Even when cars stop to take a picture with the sign inside the gate, no one in the line gets upset or impatient.

Attendance is as high as ever but, as usual, traffic slows by mid-morning. The only thing different about the festival this year is the number of artists participating and the lack of an entry fee. On the surface, anyway.

Beneath the surface, there is a current of uncertainty, even though I'm pretty sure most of us know exactly where we're headed. Even those of us who aren't ready to share yet. I watch Cujo send a text, and wonder if he'll tell me his plans or if he'll just go.

It's hard to imagine not having him in my life. We've only known each other for four years, but time moves slower in Ivydell. Feels like I've always known him. I know he grew up rough, and lived that way before he came here. Maybe for a little while after he came here, too, but he's never brought any trouble to the gate. What he does outside of it is none of my business.

There are things about his past I'll never know and might not understand even if I did, but I know he's one of the best people I've ever met.

"You ready to take a break?" I ask.

"Yeah. Feels like a good time for lunch. Let's go to my place."

"Sounds good to me. All I've got is cheese and eggs at mine." I smile, thinking about Ivy's grilled cheese sandwiches.

"A man could live on worse."

"What kind of options have you got?"

"You might want to bring your cheese and eggs."

I grab what's left of my loaf of bread before I head out for his casita, too.

There aren't as many cars parked along the road when I get back near Cujo's place, but the path is crowded with people wandering between studios and The Circle.

A photographer walks back and forth in front of Cujo's casita, pointing his camera and then lowering it before changing positions again. It seems like he's trying to get Cujo's motorcycle and the casita in the shot.

Cujo opens the door to see what the guy's doing. "You want me to move it?" he asks.

The guy with the camera looks unsure.

"Are you trying to get the bike in the shot?" Cujo asks.

"Yeah. If you really don't mind, it'd be great if you could back it up and maybe angle it a little."

Cujo nods, and starts his motorcycle. He lets the guy direct him to get in the right position.

I watch from the edge of the driveway and laugh. The guy I met four years ago wouldn't have been so accommodating, but the guy I'm watching right now understands exactly what the photographer is trying to do, and he's happy to help.

We sit on his back patio, eating sandwiches and people watching. "They all take pictures of the same things," I say.

"Yeah, but they're all seeing something different."

Ivy, Josephine, and Zara come into view. They don't see us. Ivy stops, takes off her sunglasses, and squints at the sky. I look up to see what she sees, but all I see is a few clouds. She points upward. Zara and Josephine look up and nod. They all laugh and then start walking again.

I look up again, but I still don't see anything. Cujo laughs. "One of those clouds must look like something to them," he says.

"Ah, I bet that's it. They're seeing it from a different angle."

"They always are."

If we were anyone else in any other place, now would probably feel like a good time to ask about his plans for the future. I don't, though, because we're us and we're here. Ivydell's still not the place to pry. I've asked too much already.

"What do you think?" he asks. "Maybe a few more hours at the gate, and then we call it a day?"

"We'll play it by ear. When you've had enough, you call it."

"It shouldn't be up to me," he says.

"Trust me, it'll be a joint decision. Whenever you're done, I'll be done."

"Let's go smile and wave until we're done then."

Cars arrive sporadically, but there is no afternoon rush. Day two is always busier in the morning, dying down as the day goes on, but people are leaving earlier today, too. At this rate, Ivydell will be empty before the sun goes down.

"Five o'clock," Cujo says. "Quitting time."

"Sounds good to me." Damn, this day went quick. I glance at my phone screen. "It's three o'clock."

"It's five o'clock somewhere."

"You're not wrong. You want go to the shop and lift for a while?"

"I need to make a few phone calls. Give me a couple of hours."

That sounds like more than a few phone calls. "I might have to start without you."

"That's fair."

I know my big picture plans, but there is another new possibility churning in my mind as well. A little physical exertion always helps to clear my head.

Ivy
Art Appreciation

Zara settles on a silver filagree dragonfly pendant. It's larger than my sparrow but much smaller than the pieces from Myrna's signature line.

"That's really pretty," I say.

"I love it." She rubs her fingers over it, and I smile because I do that so often to my sparrow, mapping all the curlicues and hollows with my fingertip.

"Hey, before Josephine catches up to us, I want to walk through April's studio."

"Are you sure she's there and not at The Circle?"

"No, but I have a feeling she might be."

A woman walks out of April's casita carrying a painting of Wizard sunning himself on the hood of Jensen's truck. It's funny how many obscure things are captured in the backgrounds of paintings. To everyone else who sees this woman's cat painting, that will be a cat on a random truck. I take one look at that truck, and I'm flooded with memories, so much so that I almost wish I could've bought that one.

Inside, I discover that April doesn't only paint Wizard in realistic settings. She also has mini canvases with him in fantastic costumes and doing impossible things. In one, he's driving a motorcycle. I can't be certain that's Cujo's bike, but I'd bet on it. In another, Wizard is smoking a pipe. He's immortalized with a paint brush in his paw, painting his own canvas, in a chef's hat tossing vegetables from a pan into the air, playing a piano, sitting in a lifeguard station wearing a white tank top with a red cross on it. A whistle hangs around his neck. This cat's lives are limitless.

And then I spot him pouring a glass of wine. He's wearing a pair of jeans but no shirt. That's Jensen. I know it as sure as I'm standing here. She painted him as her cat. I'm not sure if he would be flattered or concerned.

But I guess we're going to find out because there's no way I'm not buying that. I wonder if all these mini portraits are representative of someone April knows. I pick up the wine pouring Jenzard before anyone else can grab it, but I keep browsing.

April is talking to customers, but she looks over and gives me a pained smile. She's uncomfortable with me being here, but I'm genuinely here out of curiosity not animosity. I smile back and hold up the little canvas in my hand to show her which one I have. "I love this!"

Her smile softens and widens a little, and then she goes back to interacting with her customers.

"Zara, look!" I hold up another mini canvas to show her.

"Are you kidding me?" She laughs and walks over for a closer look. "Do you think this is supposed to be . . ."

I turn the canvas in my hand toward her. "Well, I'm pretty sure this is Jensen. And that's probably Cujo's bike her cat is riding over there. So, it stands to reason that this tattoo artist is exactly who you think it is."

"Yeah, he's even wearing her black boots."

"He's tattooing another cat. That's hilarious."

"Ummm, pretty sure that other cat is you."

"Why do you think that?"

"Tabby cat wearing a cropped sweater and black leggings . . . you do the math."

"Holy shit. I wonder if this really is supposed to be me and Josephine."

"If you don't buy that, I will."

"Of course I'm buying it."

When I lay the small paintings on April's kitchen counter, she stares at the them in shock "You want to buy those?"

"Yeah, they're great."

"You know they're a hundred dollars each, right?"

"Value is whatever someone is willing to pay. If that's the going rate for these, then that's the price I'll pay." I hand her my card. She pauses for a moment, and I'm afraid she might refuse to sell them to me, but she completes the transaction.

Zara and I walk back to my casita to store the little Wizard canvases safely inside with Gran's raindrop painting. "You're acquiring all kinds of art to take home with you."

"Yeah. Tawny has a painting I really want, too, but I'm afraid she may have already sold it."

"Let's go see if she's at The Circle."

Josephine catches up to us as we step onto the path. "Hey, look! It's your tattoo!"

It's the first open cactus flower I've seen since I got here. I was sure they weren't going to bloom before I had to leave, but this one is wide open and bright yellow. She's right. It's just like my tattoo.

"Go pose next to it with your tattoo out so I can take a picture for my portfolio."

A man walking ahead of us with his wife and kids looks back to watch. If he's expecting to see anything other than my hipbone, he's going to be disappointed. I tilt my hip toward the cactus bloom and pull my shorts down to show off the matching tattoo.

Josephine takes several pics. More people slow to watch us as they walk past.

"Send me all of those," I say, pulling my shorts back up.

"Of course."

Tawny is still in The Circle, but I don't see my favorite painting today either. I'm certain now that it's gone. I'll buy a different one, but I'll wait until the festival ends and choose from the pieces she has left. I like her work, but if the one that made me feel so much has already been taken, I like the rest equally. And I do like them all; the feeling's just not the same.

We watch her paint for a while, filling her on in the details from the protestors showing up this morning.

"Where will you and Leo go after you leave here?" Zara asks.

"We've got several shows and festivals scheduled throughout the summer. We live on the road more than we're home anywhere. It's how we've always been. Maybe we'll settle down somewhere one day, but we're not ready for that yet. Ivydell has been good for us, and we'll miss it. Mostly, we'll miss our friends here."

"You know you've always got a place to stay in Albuquerque," Josephine says.

"I'd love to see you at my little stretch of Texas coastline any time. I think there will probably be a room available for you near a great little biodynamic winery someday, too."

"You girls get out of here. You're making my eyes leak."

We walk back to see if Shadow's at his forge. I'm relieved to see him there. At least that means he can't get into any trouble at the gate. Dice waves when he sees us walk up. He's waving at all three of us but that glimmer in his eyes is solely for Zara. If his gaze was a glitter cannon, she'd be coated from head to toe.

When Josephine and I say we're going to walk over to Tawny and Leo's studio to see what he's got on display, Zara says she's going to stay back. No shock at all.

Leo isn't painting, but he has a casita full of people, mingling and asking questions. He's not an introvert by any means, so holding court amidst his and Tawny's paintings has him lit up with joy. It looks like he's sold a lot of their pieces. There are definitely more shoppers in here than canvases. Some of them are probably lingering solely for the coffee and the stories.

People are meant to enjoy the experience of meeting Ivydell's artists as much as the artwork they create, and Leo is as much a performer right now as he is a painter. He's a people person, good at making everyone feel at home, and these people are hanging on his every word.

I can see why people want to hang out and chat with all the artists here. Well, maybe not April since she doesn't talk much, but her artwork is interesting enough to encourage interaction. If the usual roster of artists was here, there would probably be lines at every studio.

This is different from the arts festival I used to help Gran with. When you're so close to home, it's only a brief distraction from your regular life, but when you're in the middle of the desert, you've got nowhere to rush off to. These people have all traveled just for this.

No one is thinking about going to the grocery store later or what to do about dinner when they get home or taking a kid to an activity or picking one up. They are fully present right here.

There's a light mood in the air all over Ivydell, so much less collective stress than a group this size usually exudes. The only buzz coming off the crowd is one of gentle contentment. My anxiety is practically nonexistent these days. I know it will return because I'm a worrier by nature, but I hope I can draw on the memory of this feeling after I'm gone.

I breathe in a chest full of this peaceful happiness. Times like this used to make me nervous. I'd wonder when something was going to go wrong instead of enjoying the moment. Thinking of all the moments I lost to worry, I shake my head, and then I remind myself that worrying about past worry is more pointless than the original worrying.

Looking around the room to soak in the good vibes and the vibrant art, I spot it.

Leo's just opened the closet to get a photo album from the top shelf—no doubt a visual aid for the story he's telling—and my favorite painting leans against the wall. Why is it hidden away? Maybe Tawny is saving it for another show. It might be part of a series she's working on. A gallery could be expecting it. I stare at it until he closes the door.

No sense in worrying about that any longer. I know now it's definitely not available.

Dice

Single and Ready to Mingle

Being able to turn off emotions and having an expressionless bluff always served me well at poker tables. But I never was worth a damn at hiding anything from a woman, a particularly unfortunate characteristic since my ex-wife is also a professional card player. We met at a table, and she read me like a book from that night on.

It feels good to have someone who knows you so well, until you realize it's the wrong person.

I've turned resentment that should've been reserved for my ex outward over the years since our divorce, applied it to women in general. I know it was pointless, and I let it go on far too long, depriving myself of new relationships and happiness.

I'm aware that the woman leaning her head on my shoulder as we watch Shadow bend metal is too young for me. But she's the most interesting person I've met in so long. There wasn't even a hesitant moment. As soon as I laid eyes on her, I wanted to know her.

Granted, living in Ivydell isn't exactly conducive to meeting a lot of new people, but there is something about Zara. She's clearly beautiful, but there's more to it. She's confident but not arrogant, bold but kind, independent but personable, a free spirit but grounded . . . for fuck's sake, I sound like I'm writing a greeting card about her.

I've known women since my divorce, but until Zara, there hadn't been a single one that I didn't want to slip away from before the sun came up.

She came all the way out here to visit her friend, and I've probably already taken up too much of her time, but until she turns me down cold, I'm going to keep being selfish and stealing her away every chance I get. She'll be gone soon, and I don't imagine I'll ever meet anyone else quite like her.

But I'll probably be a little more sociable in Miami because of her.

Zara has reminded me how good it can feel to spend time with a woman outside of sex. Don't get me wrong, I'm going to miss the sex with her, too, but she's easy to be around all the time. Easy to talk to, laugh with . . . well, shit, we're back to the damn greeting card aisle.

This woman probably should inspire greeting cards. The wind blows her hair into my face. I don't mind. It's soft and smells good. I'm going to miss sinking my fingers into it after she's gone.

"You want to get out of all this blowing dirt?" I ask.

"Will you rub my back when we go inside?"

"I'll rub anything you want. For as long as you need."

"How the hell are you single?" she asks, teasingly.

"The same way you are. I chose it."

She stands and extends her hand to me. "Let's go be single together for a while."

"That's an offer I'd never turn down."

Petra

The Pros of Selling Out

I NEVER IMAGINED I'D get sentimental over a damn bar of soap, but as I package up my last one, a part of me wants to keep it. It's ridiculous. I can make more soap, but letting go of this last bar today feels like taking one more step away from Ivydell.

Selling out is the best possible outcome, but I can't help wanting the last festival to go on longer. Once I'm out of merchandise, it's over for me. Soap's gone. Oils are running low. All the earmarks of a successful festival, but I guess I didn't want success this year.

If it had flopped, accepting that Ivydell had run its course might've been easier. I'm grasping for meaning, I know that.

Hell, it's a good thing I'm almost sold out. I usually close for an hour or so at a time and go check on others, but I haven't taken time out this year to see how everyone else is doing. If I close up early, I can make the rounds.

It wasn't even really my last bar. I held a few back for Ivy. Not that I can't make her more soap in the future, assuming she wants to stay in touch. I feel like she will, but if I'm wrong, I won't push myself on her.

I pull up the images of my new place on my phone. What am I going to do with all that space? It's a regular house with a big modern kitchen, a primary bathroom that I could do cartwheels in—okay, not me, but someone who could actually execute a damn cartwheel could go head-over-heels from one end to the other. Three bedrooms. I haven't even had one proper bedroom since I was in my twenties.

A swimming pool. How pathetically fucking bourgeois, right? I know, and I can't wait to dive into it every morning. I'll still be me, still living in the desert, just with more reliable air-conditioning and a dishwasher.

And that glorious pool. Selling out's not the worst thing that could happen.

A Few of Our Favorite Things

Ivy pushes open the shop door. "Knock, knock. Am I interrupting your workout?"

"Never. How'd you know I was in here?"

"Cujo stole Josephine from me, and he told me where to find you. Zara had already ditched me for Dice. I have the worst friends ever."

"In everybody's defense, we're all running out of time here."

"That's true. Are you ready to take a break?"

"You've got good timing. I haven't even started."

"Oh, I don't want to keep you from—"

I wrap my arms around her and kiss her hello. "I'd much rather work out with you."

"How do you feel about walking around with me for a while?"

"You want to play tourists, huh?"

"Well, I am one, but I want you to play one with me."

"You're not a tourist, Ivy. You just got here later than the rest of us."

"And I have to leave sooner."

"I won't be far behind you." I kiss her again. "Let's walk

around."

I take her hand in mine as we walk down the dirt road. It feels nice to be out together, and I'm looking forward to taking her out on real dates, to living a busy, full life with her in it.

She stops next to a prickly pear blossom, pulls down one side of her shorts to expose her hip bone and points to her tattoo. "Look! We match."

"Do you make a habit of pulling your pants down in public?"

"Only with you."

"What do you like besides flowers?"

"A lot of things. Wine. Popcorn . . ." She flashes me a teasing grin.

"Tell me something you like that has nothing to do with me."

"Dogs."

"Big dogs or little dogs?"

"All dogs. Candles. Fruit. All fruit. Thunderstorms. Dancing."

"Dancing, huh? I knew you had to have some flaws."

"Liking to dance is not a flaw. You don't like it?"

"Not my favorite."

"What do you like?"

"Baseball. Plain ice cream, no nuts or marshmallows or other weird shit in it. Mountains. Fire pits. Pancakes."

"How do you feel about fruit in ice cream?"

"No."

"Not even strawberries?"

"Plain ice cream."

"Weirdo. Mountains, huh?"

I squeeze her hand. "I don't want to live in the mountains, just like to visit."

"I bought a painting of you today. From April. You're a cat, but it's obviously you."

"How do you know it's me if it's a cat?"

"It's not wearing a shirt."

"But cat-me wears pants?"

"Of course. Jeans."

"Does it have my tattoos?"

"Who can tell with all that hair?"

"Right. Did you buy anything else?"

"Another cat painting of Josephine and me."

"Do you wear pants when you're a cat?"

"Black leggings."

"That does sound like you. Where the hell are you going to hang these cat paintings?"

"They're almost too small to hang, but they'll look great on little easels on the back bar at your winery. Good conversation starters."

"I'm kind of hoping people actually want to talk about my wine while they're in the tasting room."

"Well, sure, but if the conversation lags, there will be interesting cats to discuss."

"What more could one hope for?"

"Honestly, you should talk to April about licensing the one that's supposed to be you for a wine label. Did I mention cat-you is pouring wine in the painting?"

"Maybe I'll ask her if she wants to sell prints of it in the giftshop."

"They'd sell better if the image was also on one of your wine labels."

"I don't want people thinking about cat hair while they drink my wine."

"You're overthinking it."

"You might be underthinking it."

"Hey, speak of the devil!"

April's giant gray cat walks between us, almost as if he's intentionally trying to separate me from Ivy. He looks back over his shoulder and meows at me.

When we reach her casita, I lead her to the spot where she first pressed her body against mine. "This is where you initially threw yourself at me."

"And soon," she says, "there will be a monument erected to commemorate the moment. To everyone else, it will look like just another windmill, but we'll know its true meaning."

This whole area will be unrecognizable by the time the windmills go up. No signs, no casitas, no perimeter fencing. I want to believe we'd know this spot, but we won't, and it won't matter. We'll both have the memory.

"You want to come inside and light my fire?"

I grimace. "You are really bad at cheesy innuendo."

"Or am I really good at it?" She unlocks her front door. "I think you might be jealous because my cheesy lines are better than yours."

"Are you saying I don't have moves?" I follow her inside and close the door behind me.

She sits on the edge of her bed with her legs crossed, swinging her top foot like she's bored. "Show me what you've got."

I pull up a music app, press play, turn up the volume, and set my phone on her table. Taking her hands, I pull her to her feet.

"I love this song."

"I know."

"How?"

"When it came on in my truck, you turned up the volume."

"What are you doing?"

"I'm trying to dance with you. You said it was one of your favorite things. Or did I misunderstand that?"

Her body relaxes in my arms. "You understood perfectly."

I'm a little surprised that she actually lets me lead. She rests her head on my shoulder, and I wish I could set this song to play on a loop because I could spend hours holding her this close and listening to her softly singing along to a song she loves. This is a perfect moment.

Anxious knocks at her door interrupt our dance, followed by Petra's voice. "Ivy! Are you in there?"

We exchanged surprised looks. Petra sounds worried, so now I'm worried.

Ivy opens the door and Petra sighs. "Oh, good." She notices me in the background. "I'm sorry to interrupt, but I just walked through the festival and realized I hadn't seen you girls. I asked Myrna and she said she hadn't seen y'all since this morning."

"We're all fine. I left Zara at Shadow's place with Dice, and then Cujo took Josephine away from me, so I went and canceled Jensen's workout plans."

"Well, I won't keep you from the rest of your plans. See you both at The Circle later?"

"We'll be there," I say. She smiles at me. That's not the reaction she would've shown if she'd found me and Ivy alone in her casita two months ago. I return the smile.

Petra leaves, and Ivy says, "Can you restart the song?"

"As many times as you want."

Ivy

Ass Magic

I asked Jensen to play tourist and explore the last few hours of the festival with me, but once he pulled me toward my casita, I knew we were done walking around. What I didn't expect was that we'd end up dancing. Or that he'd remember a song I turned up the volume for in his truck.

I've never known anyone who paid attention to the small things the way he does. I didn't even remember hearing that song in his truck until he mentioned it, but I'll never forget dancing with him this afternoon.

Even I can only listen to this song so many times, though. It's so easy for him to surprise me, and I don't think I'm that easily impressed. Still, it feels strange to have someone know me so well so soon. I wouldn't do anything to sabotage what's building between us, but I've always liked being the one who could shock my partner in a relationship.

Jensen doesn't shock easily, though. Or if he does, he hides it well. I wonder if he'd be shocked to know that I took a striptease workshop with some friends when I was in college. When I've undressed for him, my moves weren't entirely adlibbed.

"Turn off your music. I want to use mine now."

After he turns off the song we've been dancing to, I tell him to take a seat on the bed.

"So, you know how I take my clothes off in a very deliberate way when you're watching me undress?"

"I have an immense appreciation for the way you undress."

"Well, I've had a little training."

"Meaning?"

"As a stripper." I leave it at that to see his reaction.

"You? A stripper? Huh, tell me more."

No judgement. No shock. Just *tell me more*, like he knows there's more to the story.

"Okay, it wasn't my job, but I took a few classes. And I performed once at an amateur night with several of the women from the workshop."

"Wow. So, there could be a video online of you stripping."

"Don't say that!" I laugh. "I spent way too long worrying about that after I did it. The place was pretty strict about their *no phones* policy, though. Plus, it was almost seven years ago."

Taking that workshop made me feel so much more confident taking off my clothes, but I feel way more apprehensive taking my clothes off in front of Jensen right now than I ever did before. I'm not ashamed that I took the classes or that I performed for a whole scandalous three minutes on a stage in an actual club, but now that I've revealed this fun fact about myself, I'm worried he'll be critiquing my moves. That he'll be expecting something more exciting than I'm able to deliver.

Might as well have fun with it at this point. I start the music on my phone. "It was striptease and pole dancing, but obviously, I don't have a pole here."

He pulls out his phone.

"I'm sorry, sir. You'll have to put your phone away. No filming or photography is allowed."

"I'm just making a note to add a pole to my office at the winery."

I rock the hem of my tank top up a few inches at a time, waiting for the beat to pick up before I attempt to dramatically pull it over my head and whip it around a few times before tossing it at him. It gets hung in my hair. In an effort to save my sexy opening maneuver, I try to seductively roll my head from side-to-side while pulling on the shirt, hoping it will release itself, but somehow, I'm twisting it further into my hair. What's happening? Fuck it. I leave it hanging there. I'm sure it'll fall out on its own—maybe at the perfect moment and this will all look intentional. It could happen.

My fingers slip under my waistband, and I roll my hips as I begin to slide my jogging shorts down my thighs. When my shorts reach my knees, I let them drop, and lift a foot to step out of them. Jensen bites back a smile, but he's still watching me intently. My second foot snags the leg hole and instead of leaving the shorts on the floor, drags them across it. Nothing hotter than frantically shaking your foot like a baby alligator is trying to bite your toes off. The shorts fall to the floor again.

Could I have simply used my toes to teasingly fling my shorts at him? Absolutely could have. Absolutely did not. Why are my clothes attacking me? I wasn't this bad on the very first night of the workshop.

If I were on a stage, I'd be getting booed. Jensen licks his lips and frees his smile. He's not laughing at me yet, so I think I still have a chance to save this from becoming a comedy routine.

I reach around and unhook my bra, letting the straps slide down my arms. Holding the cups to my body, I bend forward and shimmy, lifting my body from the lace in my hands little by little and then dropping the bra completely as I stand up. Yay! This move works like it's supposed to!

His eyebrows lift appreciatively. It will never cease to amaze me how a man can see your bare breasts a million times and still look at them like he's never had the privilege before. They way his eyes map the swells and then zero in on my nipples is all the boost my ego needs to feel much better about my performance.

When I lift my hair with my arms rising above my head to pull my tits higher, I'm reminded that my shirt is still stuck, which is going to ruin the dramatic waterfall of my hair when I slide my fingers through the tips. Whatever. The front sections will still cascade back onto my shoulders.

He pulls out his wallet, and I laugh. I never anticipated earning pity tips. Dancing closer to see where he'll put it, I shake my head with a little extra force. The shirt clings to my hair like Velcro.

Jensen tucks a bill into the top of my panties, and then he motions for me to turn around. Dammit. I don' t want to turn around and showcase the twisted shirt stuck in my hair. I ignore his request and attempt to straddle his leg. He pushes me back. "Are you not working for tips tonight, sweetheart?" He repeats the signal of his hand.

We're really going to role-play this, I guess. Okay then. I bite my lip, lower my lashes bashfully, and turn around for him.

His hands easily free my shirt in seconds. I glance over my shoulder and mouth *thank you*. He smiles and says, "Show me your appreciation." He smacks my butt. "Work this pretty ass for me."

"You're not allowed to touch the dancers. You must've missed the announcement. And the signs."

"You must've missed my VIP badge." He points to his chest, but my eyes go instantly to his scorpion tattoo. Just the way they did when we first met.

"Does that tattoo mean anything?"

He pulls a twenty from his wallet. "Does this mean anything to you?"

Oh, he's fully committed to being an alpha-hole in the club, huh? Hmmm, I could get into performing for this arrogant, attractive guy. "Not much, actually. Got anything with any greater meaning?"

His wicked smile tells me he likes the direction I'm taking his game. He pulls out two more crisp twenties and flicks all three bills across my ass.

If that striptease workshop taught me anything, it's that I cannot twerk. I mean, I really, really cannot do it. Like my ass cheeks turn to stone the moment I try. But I've baited him, and if I refuse now, the super-charged tension in the air between us will fizzle.

He won't be the first guy whose fantasy of a statuesque, red-haired seductress goes up in flames when he realizes I've got the moves of an actual statue when my nerves take over.

I know how it's supposed to work: feet apart, bend low, hands above the knees, weight forward, lower back arched and booty pop, booty pop, booty pop, and just keep going until the magic happens. The instructor would always tell me to separate my butt cheeks from my body, let them move on their own, but mine are firmly attached, both literally and metaphorically. I was not gift with a magical ass.

Maybe the four-thousandth-nine-hundredth-eighty-eighth time is the charm? If it doesn't work, I'll just roll my hips around and back up until I can grind against his thigh. When all else, fails, dry hump his leg. The instructor never actually said that, but she did say improvising can save you from making a fool of yourself.

Tossing him a quick impish smile over my shoulder, I squat with my feet shoulder-width apart, arch my lower back, plant my hands on my thighs just above my knees, arch my back a little more, take a breath and wait for the beat, and then booty pop, booty pop, booty pop . . . it's not happening. My whole butt is thrusting but it's all fused—my hips, my lower back, my ass. A statue. No wiggle, no jiggle.

Weight forward. Oh, right. Gotta transfer more weight to the balls of my feet. Gotta trust . . .

It feels like you'll fall, but you won't. You've got this. Trust. Separate your cheeks. Let them move freely. Take more weight off your heels. Booty pop, booty pop, weight forward, let your cheeks move, booty pop, booty pop, weight forward, ass up and back, pop, pop, pop—

That's it. This is happening.

My weight shifts forward. All of it. And my bowling ball ass is about to be a wrecking ball. Every part of me is moving freely as I scramble to regain my balance. All the wrong gyrations.

I go down in slow motion, yet somehow, it's over in the fraction of a second.

Fuck, this tile is hard.

Jensen launches himself off the bed. "Are you okay?" He helps me sit up on the floor, and sits next to me, checking my wrists and ankles for sprains like he's a trained medic.

"Yeah, I think I'm fine. I'm sorry, but my ass just can't work magic."

He laughs himself to tears, which does wonders for my ego. "Ivy, trust me, you have the most magical ass I've ever seen. All of you is magic."

"I can't twerk."

"Not at all." He wipes more tears from his eyes. "But you didn't need to."

"You said to show you what my ass could do."

"So, you picked the one thing you knew it absolutely couldn't?"

I slap his chest. "I hate you."

He grabs my wrists and kisses my fingers. "No, you don't. But, seriously, are you hurt anywhere?"

"No, I don't think so. I'll probably have a few bruises tomorrow."

"It might not take that long."

"Great."

He carries me to my bed. "Do you need ice?"

I roll my ankles and wrists, bend my arms and legs. "No. Stop staring at me. I know I look like an idiot."

"You look beautiful." He kisses my forehead.

"Leave my sixty bucks on the table."

More tears roll down his face as he laughs. "You earned every cent, but I'm not leaving yet. Unless you're kicking me out."

"You can stay, but you have to be nice to me."

"I'll do anything you want."

"Will you hand me my shirt?"

"Except that."

"You know, the amount of time I'm naked while you're fully clothed is starting to feel disproportionate."

"You're right. You should be naked far more often. Roll over."

"Wow. No effort at seduction at all. I guess the honeymoon's over."

"I was going to rub your back."

I flip like a pancake. No further questions.

His hands are so big and warm. I wonder if he took a massage workshop. He definitely has magic hands. When they reach my ass, I'm so relaxed that my cheeks move freely under his palms. There is no tension left in my body.

He slides my panties down and I pop my ass to make it easier for him to remove them—lower back arched, weight forward. As soon as he has them on the floor, my feet spread shoulder-width apart, but I remain flat on my stomach.

My body melts into the mattress when he massages my naked ass. His skin feels amazing on mine, but I fully expect him to give in to temptation and spank at any second. He slides a hand between my legs instead. I'm drenched, and he spreads my arousal everywhere before he pinches my clit between his fingers and rolls it until I moan. "Fuck me."

"You haven't come yet."

"You can owe me one. I just want to feel you inside me."

He takes off his clothes without leaving the bed, and then he rolls his naked body on top of mine, sinking me further into the mattress. His weight holding me down doesn't feel oppressive; it feels protective. When he presses his cock inside my pussy without separating our bodies, it feels erotic.

My face slides on the pillow as he rocks his weight forward, burying his full length in me. His arms slide up to frame mine until they form double goal posts. He holds my wrists and kisses my shoulder as he slowly fucks me.

I'm trapped beneath him, but I know he'd give me more space

if I asked for it. He'd change to any position I wanted, but I want this one. I want to be pinned under his body, to feel him rolling his hips, forcing me to take every inch of his cock, to know when I whimper at his deepest thrust, he understands that I don't want him to stop because he knows my sounds and can read my body's reactions.

Relaxing fully, I savor the way he's driving into me. Trust.

I can't move, can't pop my hips back to meet his thrusts, or touch myself. He uses his jaw to brush my hair aside, so he can bite at the base of my neck. I squirm, and he increases his hold on my wrists, bites again while grinding his hips against my ass.

My juices flood the comforter. He groans, still hitting the spot that just made me squirt on his dick. I float for a moment, detached from everything as the release flows from my body.

"God, I love when you do that."

"I love when you make me do that. Might need to borrow your dryer later."

His voice comes out in a gravelly sexy tone so deep it almost hurts my ears. It sounds the way his stubbled jaw feels if it drags downward, abrading the smoothness of my inner thigh. "I'm not done with this pussy yet."

"That's why I said later. I'm not ready for you to be done with me yet."

"You like being my good little slut?" He rams into me, lifting my hips off the mattress.

"I love being your private whore." My breath is ragged. "Love the way you use me."

His hips lunge in an uncontrolled thrust. His thighs tighten against mine, and his shoulders shudder at my back. I contract my pelvic floor as much as I can with my pussy full of his dick, locking my walls around him, and his moan is a heady mix of ecstasy and angst. He drills into me with rhythmic grunts until his orgasm erupts.

I clutch fistfuls of the comforter as his hands clench tighter around my wrists.

When he's finished and his body stills, he slides off me and lies propped on his elbow at my side, playing with my hair. "I didn't hurt your wrists, did I?"

"No. I would've told you if I needed you to ease up. I didn't hurt your dick, did I?" I tease.

"Only in all the best ways. Roll onto your back so I can make you feel good."

"I already made a pretty big mess."

"Yeah, but that was spontaneous. I love it when that happens, but I want to you to enjoy a more deliberately delivered pleasure now."

"Hey, you're a grown man. I'm not here to put limitations on you."

I roll over and he scoots closer to me. He's laughing at my comment. No tears this time. He lifts and kisses my hands one at a time, inspecting them for bruising or swelling. He doesn't say he's doing that, but he is. "I love you."

"I love you, too."

His hand massages my swollen pussy, pulling the mixture of my release and his up to lubricate around my clit, circling it with a firm pressure. It's tender, and I don't think it's going to take him long to get me off, though part of me wants to prolong it.

He lowers his head to kiss my chest, trailing his mouth down until it claims my hard nipple. His warm tongue lashes over it, and I no longer want to prolong anything. The dual stimulation is too good to deny.

"You always know just how to touch me."

"If I ever don't, tell me. I'll always give you what you need."

I believe him. And belief is the better part of magic.

The Spirit Sisters

Tea Time

"How's your tea, Elma?"

"It's fine. We're going to miss this place, sister."

"And the spirits who stay behind."

"Yes, but, Alma, you know spirit does as spirit likes."

"I do indeed."

"Do you suppose we will see some of these people again?"

"Oh, I certainly hope so. But we will be far from Texas soon."

"As will some of them."

"True, Elma. That is true. But paths do cross in new places."

"We have delivered many messages in this desert."

"We will be messengers wherever we go."

"Alma, I know we've never been big TV watchers, but I think I would like to watch his show."

"You watch it and tell me about it, sister. I'm afraid it might be too rough for me. I just don't care for violence."

"Nor do I, but it's all make believe. And I don't think we've ever met a TV star before they became one."

"You're right about that, Elma. Most of them are probably more likeable in their pre-star life, but I don't think it will change him much."

"No, Alma, I don't imagine it will."

"The spirits are reconvening."

"Yes, I hear them, too, sister. But there's still time to finish our tea. There is always time for tea."

Jensen

Smells Like Rain

There is a gentle breeze at The Circle tonight. Cujo, Shadow, and Dice play to Ivydell residents only. No festival goers remain.

The festival is officially over for good. I'm not even sure how much cleanup we'll do tomorrow. Petra made comments about leaving it all for the new owners to take care of. They're going to clear everything, anyway. But she could wake up tomorrow and decide we need to clean Ivydell, regardless.

It's mostly just signs, but no matter how many extra trash receptacles we provide, some people insist on littering. Whatever Petra wants us to do, we'll do. There will be the dinner tomorrow night as usual, but after that, nothing about Ivydell will be the same. When the seasonal residents leave this time, they're never coming back.

Zara leaves on Tuesday.

And then Ivy hits the road on Friday morning. My gut retches every time I think about watching her drive away. It doesn't matter that I won't be long behind her. I was sure I wanted to wait until the bitter end to leave, but the closer it gets to Ivy leaving, the more I feel ready to go.

I feel a responsibility to stay and help Petra, Myrna, and the spooky sisters pack up, make sure they get on the road safely, but I feel a burning need to look out for Ivy, too.

"Wanna dance?" Her eyes sparkle in the moonlight.

"I never want to miss an opportunity to dance with you."

Josephine makes gagging noises, and Zara laughs.

No one else is dancing, but it doesn't take Tawny and Leo long to join us. Then Petra and Myrna. Zara pulls Josephine to the center. The only ones left sitting are April and the spooky sisters, but I don't know that any of them would accept an invitation if it were offered.

April's cat doesn't wait to be invited. The giant fluffball winds between Ivy and me. It's all I can do not to trip over him. Thankfully, he moves on to bother every pair. I hold Ivy closer until the last note plays.

Thunder rolls in the distance. We could use a good cleansing storm. I hope it rains all night.

Dice packs up his guitar and heads straight for Zara. "Is it girls' night, tonight?"

She looks at Ivy like she's not sure how to respond.

"I'm too exhausted to be any fun tonight, anyway," Ivy says. "But you're mine all day tomorrow."

She turns to Josephine, "You, too. Unless you're leaving for Albuquerque."

"Not until Tuesday. I don't want to miss the community dinner tomorrow night."

"Will you be back on Thursday?"

"No. I'm working through the rest of the week to make up for the extra days I took off."

"So, you and Zara are both leaving Tuesday morning. Yeah, you're definitely both all mine tomorrow."

With that decided, Zara walks off with Dice, and Josephine with Cujo. I expect more people to hang around, but everyone walks away, leaving Ivy and me alone in The Circle.

"You want to sit and look at the stars for a while?" I ask.

"Yeah. I do."

I sit on a bench and she lays on her back with her head resting on my lap. I play with her hair while she stares at the sky. "Are you afraid?" she asks.

"Of leaving here? No. I'm ready. Looking forward to it, actually."

"But are you afraid that we won't be the same away from here?"

"No. I think you are the most genuine person I've ever met, and I can't imagine a place changing you."

"This place changed me."

"It changed me, too. But so did you. If you stop changing, you stop growing, so I guess I don't want either of us to stay the same. I want us to grow together. We'll change in good ways. Together."

"You sound so sure."

"Are you having doubts?"

"Not because I don't want to be with you. I just can't let go of worry completely."

"You can worry as much as you need to, as long as you promise to talk to me. Let me know what you're worrying about."

"It's probably always going to be something."

"I'm always going to want to know. I might not always be able to help, but I want to know. Always."

The wind picks up and soft rain starts to fall. Ivy sits up. "Kiss me one more time before we go."

I kiss her. "I still have a few more days to kiss you everywhere."

We hold hands on the walk back to Sparrow's Song. It's closer than my casita, and the rain is starting to come down harder.

"Shower with me. I'll wash your hair."

"If that's code for anything, you're going to be disappointed because I am truly exhausted."

"No code."

She looks so gorgeous with warm water cascading over her body. Like a dream come true. I wash her hair, loving the way it feels in my hands. As soon as I've rinsed it, she hands me a bottle of conditioner. "Now this. You have to coat my hair and it has to stay on for five minutes."

"Anything for another five minutes of being pampered."

"Exactly."

I coat her hair with conditioner and pull her body close to mine. "I'm going to hold you and breathe in this herbal steam for five minutes, and then we're going to forget about the calendar, and sleep like we have all the tomorrows in the world."

"You could rub my back. I mean, since your hands are there, anyway."

"Brat. One-hundred percent brat." I rub her soft skin. It's slick from the conditioner running down from her hair.

"I'm maybe sixty-percent brat at most."

"Ninety-nine-point-nine."

"I can see I'm going to be the voice of reality in this couple."

"Whatever you need to believe."

The wind is blowing harder by the time we're dried off and ready for bed. Ivy opens her front door. "So that's why it's not flying open and shut. Why didn't you tell me you'd put a latch on my screen door?"

"I didn't need a round of applause. You wanted a latch, and I told you I'd get you one, so I did. I'm not perfect, and I'll piss you off in a million different ways on a million different days, but you can count on me to do what I say I will. You can depend on me, Ivy. I can promise you that much."

"Thank you."

"And you never have to say thank you. But you're welcome. Close the door. It's raining."

"In a minute. I want to smell the rain before I go to sleep."

I wrap my arms around her and smell the rain with her for a minute before I close the door and take her to bed. There is nothing quite like the smell of the desert when it rains. And there is no other woman quite like her.

Ivy

Stars on the Horizon

Everyone slept in today. The rain made it cozy, but it's stopped now, and the afternoon sun is warm. More cactus blooms are open, and everything looks bright and beautiful. There is no dust blowing in the air, just a clear, fresh breeze.

Jensen and Cujo are helping Tawny and Leo get food ready for tonight. They won't let anyone else help in the Community Center, but we're all welcome to prepare something in our own casitas to share.

I grabbed Zara and Josephine as soon as I woke up, and we all went to the grocery store together. I have Gran's potato salad recipe committed to memory, and the potatoes are already cooked and cooling on my counter.

Josephine is making a mediterranean salad with greens and grains. Her casita smells like fresh peppers, tomatoes, and herbs. We're rotating between all three of our places, helping each other. Okay, we don't really need help with our dishes, but we're helping to keep each other's wine glasses refilled. Our doors are open, and it's a perfect day.

The smell of baking cookies wafts from Myrna's casita.

All of Ivydell smells delicious.

Wood smoke rises from behind the Community Center. The

guys are preparing to grill meats and fish.

Zara insists on making homemade mac and cheese for everyone. She wouldn't accept that she didn't need to contribute because she's a guest. Zara is always a contributor. Our casitas have small ovens, but she's preparing a pan to go in my oven, Josephine's and hers. No one will go without mac and cheese tonight. And no one will forget her once they taste it. Of course, Dice will remember her for much more.

"So, you really don't think you'll see Dice after you leave here?" Josephine asks, leaning against Zara's counter.

"I don't know. Maybe I'll go to Miami if he invites me. We'll see." She strains the first pot of pasta in her sink. Everything has to be done in batches in such a small kitchen, but we've got time. "What about you and Cujo? You'll still see each other, right?"

"Well, it'll be hard not to see him when he's living in my apartment." She laughs for a second before she realizes what she's said. "Shit."

"Oh, no you don't," I say. "You can't just say that and then pretend you didn't. Cujo is moving to Albuquerque to live with you?"

"No. I mean, yes, he's moving there. And yes, he's going to live with me. But I'm not the reason he's moving there."

"That makes no sense," Zara says. "Explain it."

"I can't."

"What do you mean you can't?" I top off her wine again, figuring maybe a little more vino might loosen her lips enough for us to get the whole story.

She looks at her glass and shakes her head at me. "It's not for me to tell. It's up to him when and what he tells anyone about his plans."

"Okay, I can respect that," I say.

"Bullshit," Zara says. "We're not going to tell him we know anything. What's the big mystery?"

Josephine won't give us anything more. Finally, Zara says, "Okay, fine. But if he hasn't told everyone by the time you and I pull out tomorrow morning, you have to tell me. He'll never know you said a word. He and I will probably never see each other again, so it doesn't matter if you tell me."

"That's called rationalization," Josephine says.

"Yeah, and you need to be rational." Zara pours her melted cheese mixture over of a pan full of pasta and stirs it. It smells fantastic, and it hasn't even baked yet.

"I'm hungry. Let's eat our tacos now." We stopped at the taco stand that Josephine and I hit coming and going on our trip to Albuquerque.

We all walk across the street to my casita where we left our bag full of tacos. Zara puts a pot of water on to boil in my kitchen for her second batch of pasta. After we eat and her pasta is strained in my sink, she takes it back to her place to make another round of her cheese sauce. She'll bring the pan back over to go in my oven, so I preheat it for her.

Josephine goes next door to put her salad together, and I stay behind to mix up Gran's potato salad.

I've never made it by myself before. I've helped her chop and mix it since I was old enough to be any help at all, but even when I was too little to use a knife and not strong enough to mix it well, she always called me into the kitchen to give it a final stir, saying it needed a little bit more love, and she knew I'd add just the right amount.

For years, my stir would be nothing more than barely dragging a spoon over the surface, but she would assure me I'd made it perfect. After I was an adult, she still insisted I needed to give it a final stir to mix in a little more love.

Today, the love in it is all mine, but I step away from the bowl before I cover it to go into the fridge. I can envision her here, giving it one more loving stir so it will be just right. It's silly, but it feels necessary to me.

Zara brings two pans of mac and cheese over, one for my oven and one for Josephine's. We walk next door to start the third pan cooking, and to see if Josephine needs any help, aka to see if she will cave and tell us why Cujo is moving to Alburquerque if not for her.

We ask once more, but then we let it go. After all, prying goes against Ivydell's unwritten code of conduct. And I don't really want to piss Cujo off. I like the teddy bear side of him.

Petra stops by with her wagon, and we load all our food into it. Myrna walks out of Wild Sage, carrying a large container of cookies and a bottle of wine. I've put a few bottles in the wagon, and I know Jensen went to Hilltop this morning to get more.

I already know this dinner is going to be a party.

Everything is great, and I eat way too much. We all do. The guys play and Cujo sings. And then we all sit around and eat more dessert.

Jensen sets his beer on the table. "Okay, spill it," he says.

Cujo narrows his eyes at him.

"No, I'm serious. You're in a room full of people who love you and want to know what your future holds. Don't keep us all in the dark, worried about you.”

“Worried about me? There’s no reason for anybody to worry about me.”

The Spirit Sisters giggle. Um, I know it’s past their bedtime, but they are not the giggly type. They don’t drink, so it’s not a tipsy giggle. I’ve heard a chuckle from one of them, but only after she shared a prediction with me.

“They know, don’t they?” I ask before I can think better of it.

Both twins cover their mouths and look away.

Cujo smiles at the old women. He has a soft spot for Alma and Elma. He won’t get mad at them. “I guess they might.” He tips his beer back and takes a long drink.

We all watch him.

“Aw, hell. Fine. But I don’t want to hear any shit about it. I mean it. None.”

Jensen leans forward with his forearms crossed on the table. “Oh, this must be good.”

“Several months ago, I was in Albuquerque visiting Jojo, and I went to the store while she was with a client. This woman came up to me and asked if I was talent.” He throws his arms in the air to demonstrate his confusion. “I didn’t know what the hell she meant, so I told her I played guitar and sang a little. She goes, ‘No. I mean are you an actor?’ and I shook my head like she was crazy.”

“Holy shit,” Dice says as he and Jensen exchange looks.

“Hey, you want me to finish telling this story or not?”

“Yes!” we all yell.

“I tell her I’m not an actor. So, then she wants to know if I’m a biker. I hedge, tell her that’s a long story. She says speaking of stories about bikers, she’s a casting director for a new TV series about a motorcycle club. And according to her, I've got the perfect look for one of the leads they're having trouble casting. She asks if I'd be willing to come in and read for the part."

We're all exchanging looks now. This is wilder than anything I might've imagined.

"At this point, I'm kind of amused by it and figure why the hell not? Jojo had a full day booked, and I didn't have anything else to do. Right away, I see they've got some shit wrong. I mean, I know it's fiction, and it won't be entirely accurate, but they had some big problems. I gave them pointers, helped out with the specifics so they wouldn't look entirely stupid when the show aired, and they listened. Asked me more questions. By the time I read for the part, I think they'd already decided it was mine."

Jensen stands up. "You're telling me you're going to be a fucking TV star?"

"Nobody said anything about being a star. They've only got one season approved. Ten episodes. That may be all there ever is."

"Is that where you've been going when you stay gone for so long? You've been filming?" Jensen asks.

"That and taking some classes."

"Acting lessons?" Dice asks, unable to keep the amusement from his voice.

"You got a problem with that?" Cujo asks.

"No, man. I think it's great."

Shadow loses it at the end of the table. The old man laughs so hard he can hardly breathe. He pounds on the table. "That's the funniest damn shit I've ever heard. Look at you, Hollywood."

Cujo laughs. No way he'd get mad at Shadow. The guys all stand and walk toward him. He starts waving his hands to push them back.

"Stand your ass up," Jensen says.

"You must be feeling big tonight," Cujo says, but he stands.

They all step forward, taking turns hugging him, patting him on the back, and congratulating him.

"You win, man," Dice says, running his hand through his hair. "You win for the most interesting plans after Ivydell."

When the men step away, the women all take a turn hugging him and telling him how cool we think his opportunity is. He allows it, but he's uncomfortable with all the attention.

"Good thing I was planning on buying a damn TV," Petra says, smacking him on the shoulder.

"Can you imagine if any of us had just turned on our TV one night and seen him?" Myrna asks. "Were you going to tell us eventually or just risk us having a heart attack?"

Cujo smiles.

"What's the name of the show?" I ask.

He rolls his eyes before he answers. "The Basin Brotherhood. I didn't have any say in the name."

"Hey," Jensen says. "It's not based on a real club, right? You going to be okay doing this?"

Cujo nods. "Purely fiction. It's all good. I'm covered."

I'm not exactly sure what the exchange meant, but I know I'm not the only worrier in this relationship.

"Well," Petra says. "That makes three of us who will be in New Mexico, so if any of you pass through, you've got no excuses not to call a mini reunion dinner."

"You'll be in Albuquerque, too?" I ask.

"No. Santa Fe, but that's not far."

Everyone else begins to share their immediate plans. It's nice to hear where everyone is headed next. I like knowing that Petra will be close to Josephine and Cujo.

Jensen shares more about his plans for the winery, and then without warning, he announces that I'll be managing the tasting room and handling all the marketing. I did accept his offer, and I'm excited about it, but it's weird to hear it officially announced.

I haven't even told Mom yet. She's going to think I lost my damn mind in the desert.

Everyone gasps, and then the congratulations begin, along with more questions, most of which I can't even answer.

After we've cleaned up and put away the leftover food, I ask Zara if she's staying with Dice tonight. She says they already said their goodbyes. "I was hoping to hang out with you, but I totally understand if you're staying with your boss."

"Hey, don't call him that. Especially not loud enough for him to hear. Of course, I want to spend your last night here with you."

I kiss Jensen and tell him Zara and I are calling it a night. He drives us to my casita. We could've easily walked, but he wouldn't hear it because we were leaving before everyone else.

We sit up wide awake in my bed, watching through my patio doors for falling stars. "Do you think I'm crazy?" I ask. "I've only known him for eight weeks."

"Yeah, but do the math. If you'd only known him for eight weeks at home, you'd probably both have full-time jobs, so you'd only see each other maybe a few times during the week and once on the weekend because you'd have to do your household chores and run errands, right? So, that's what? Maybe five times a week at the most and only for a few hours, so let's say fifteen waking hours a week to be generous. How many hours a week do you spend with him here?"

"A lot more than fifteen. We've probably spent that much time together over just a few days. Sometimes in one day."

"See! That's what I'm saying. Eight weeks in Ivydell time is like a year in the real world. And plenty of people our age made big life decisions with someone after a year. Hell, you can make a whole baby in less time."

"I freaking love you." I know her math has oversimplified the situation by a lot, but Jensen and I have spent way more time together than we would've if we'd met outside Ivydell. She's right on the surface, and I feel better about everything when I consider it from this perspective. It hasn't been a normal eight weeks. It hasn't been a year, either, but it's been longer than people could understand if they've never lived here.

A shooting star zips through our field of view. "Make a wish!" I shout.

She squeezes her eyes shut. When she opens them, she asks if I made one, too.

"No, I've made several wishes since I came here. That star was all yours."

Jensen

Shared Wishes

I GET UP EARLY to help Ivy see Zara off. "If you have any trouble on the road, call us," I say. "I'll get to you as quick as I can."

"I have roadside assistance, but I appreciate the offer."

"Okay, but if you do need anything, we're here."

I'm probably offering too much, but watching Ivy tell her friend goodbye and seeing how hard this is for her, even knowing she's going to see her again in less than a week . . . it just reenforces that I'm going to lose my mind between the time Ivy leaves and I get to see her again.

"You working today?" I ask as Zara drives away.

"No. Tawny asked me to come over for coffee at their casita this morning. Leo's opening the coffee shop in the Community Center, but she said she wanted to see me alone."

"Okay. Well, if you're free later, let me know. I'm going to go lift for a while and then see if Petra's changed her mind about cleaning up after the festival."

We kiss, and I realize this could be a normal occurrence someday in the not-too-distant future. I'll be able to kiss her hello and goodbye every day. It's what I want.

Petra stands by her decision that we're not bothering to clean up signs, says she and Myrna have already picked up the trash. I should've known.

Cujo comes up to the shop to lift, and I don't give him too much shit about his acting gig. I get a few jabs in, but he laughs them off.

"Hey, when do you have to be in Albuquerque?"

"Not for five weeks." He wipes sweat from his brow. "Why?"

"I need a favor."

"Another one? Haven't I been doing you favors since I met your skinny ass?"

I laugh. "Probably, but I'd really appreciate this one. How do you feel about the beach?"

Ivy works for a few hours after she meets with Tawny, but we make plans for an early dinner. There's enough food leftover from last night to feed us all for the rest of the week, and everybody else will probably have dinner together in the Community Center until it's gone, but I want to take Ivy out. She's sad about Josephine leaving this morning, too.

"Fourth best barbecue in the state?" she asks when she climbs into my truck.

"No. Let's just ride a while, find someplace different."

"We might have to ride for a long time."

"You got other plans?"

"Nope. I'm all yours."

"I love the sound of that. What did Tawny want?"

"She gave me the painting."

"I had a feeling she was going to do that."

"She wouldn't let me pay for it, but I saw the prices on her other paintings during the festival. It's a huge gift."

"Accept it. She did it because she wanted to."

"I know, and I love it so much. She said the fact that I loved it so much was all the payment she needed."

"She meant that. I know Tawny. Is it going to be another one for the winery?"

"I don't know. I may want to keep this one at home."

"She'd want you to hang it wherever you'll get the most enjoyment out of it. There won't be a winery to hang it in for a while, anyway."

"That's true. I can hang it home, and then decide if I want to move it when the time comes to decorate Vintage Vibes."

We find a hole-in-the-wall diner nearly two and half hours away from Ivydell. I've never been out this way, just took a chance. The food is simple, but the pie is incredible.

"I feel like I've gained ten pounds in the past week." She drops her fork, and leans against the back of the booth.

"You're perfect." I lean across the table to feed her the last bite of my chocolate pie.

She shoves the saucer with the rest of her apple pie toward me. "Finish that. I don't want to eat again for three days."

I roll the windows down on the way back to Ivydell. She falls asleep and stays that way the last hour of the drive.

We spend the night at my place.

WEDNESDAY, SHE WORKS IN the morning, and we fish in the afternoon. I want to spend time with her, but I also want to keep her mind off the other goodbyes she'll have to say soon. Neither of us catches anything, but I wouldn't want to be anywhere else.

We stay at my place again.

BY THURSDAY, I WANT every minute of her time, but Petra and Myrna steal her away for a hike. I should've hiked with her while she was here. Can't believe we never did that. Time flies.

We have dinner with everyone. She says her goodbyes to the Spirit Sisters before they go back to their casita. They've had several late nights, and they're ready to turn in early. I didn't expect her to get so emotional saying goodbye to these women. She'll be a mess tomorrow morning. I hate the thought of her driving when she's upset.

I've pulled up all the casita signs and stored them in my shop. It upset Ivy to see hers gone already. If I'd known taking it early would have that kind of impact, I'd have left it.

We stay and visit with everyone for hours after dinner, but eventually, people start to leave. No one wants to say goodbye to her, and I suspect most of them will be out front to say goodbye to her all over again in the morning.

I walk her over to the shop to get the Sparrow's Song sign. "This is yours," I say. "I was always going to give it to you. I'd planned to bring it to the beach to surprise you, but I don't want you to leave here thinking I'm such an asshole that I'd really take your sign."

She bursts into tears. "I didn't think you were an asshole, but I really did want it."

"I know." I hold her until she stops crying.

"This is so stupid. I'm crying at everything."

"You're allowed to have feelings, Ivy."

She makes me put the sign back in front of her casita for her last night.

We stay at Sparrow's Song on her last night.

Dawn breaks Friday morning, and she's sleeping so soundly. I know she set an alarm, and I can't bear to wake her before it goes off, so I watch her sleep. A sliver of sunlight lights up a section hair that falls over her cheek. This is the last time I'll ever see her in this bed.

We packed her car last night before dinner. The only things left to take are her suitcase and her sign from out front. I slip outside to load that for her while she sleeps.

Before I go back inside, I take her little amethyst angel ghost from my pocket and set her on the dash, staring into the car.

Ivy rolls over and opens her eyes when I come back into the casita. "My alarm just went off," she says.

"Looks like it's going to be a clear day."

"Good. At least there's that." She half-smiles, and tumbles out of bed. I want her to walk straight into my arms, but I understand when she goes to the bathroom and turns on the shower. If we start our emotional goodbye now, she won't get on the road until this afternoon.

We agreed to not use the word goodbye today, not between us. The plan is for me to be at the beach in less than a month. That gives her time to settle back into her place, have some space to herself, and decide when she wants to leave her job, to be sure about everything. It's a good plan, probably the smartest way to handle things.

I sit on the edge of her bed and stare at the wall while she finishes getting ready. When she zips up her suitcase, I take it out to her car. "Come out whenever you're ready," I say before I close her door.

"Thanks."

Petra has told everyone they can take anything they want from their casitas when they go. They're going to be demolished. I had big plans to chip out Saltillo tiles from several casitas to use somewhere in the winery, but ultimately decided against it. There's nothing from my casita I want, but knowing Ivy, she may come out with something too big to fit in her car.

I lean against her hood and smile. It's such a beautiful morning.

She walks out with her arms full. "You need pillows?"

"I don't need them, but I want them. I can sleep on mine and put the one you slept on next to it, and whenever I look over, I can imagine you there. I know you want to laugh at me right now, but it'll help."

"I don't want to laugh at you, Ivy. Give me a ride home?"

"Sure. Hop in, lazy."

She stuffs her pillows in the back, and I settle into the passenger seat with adrenaline buzzing like hornets in veins. This is it. The end of our time together in Ivydell.

"She can ride in the console." The amethyst woman loses her spot on the dash. Ivy cuts her eyes at me as she starts the car. "You just had to do it one last time, didn't you?"

"Oh, you have a lifetime of that to look forward to."

She laughs. It feels good to be able to make her laugh right now.

Sure enough, everyone is standing in front of the Community Center, ready to give Ivy a friendly send-off. Even Shadow came up to tell her goodbye again. Tawny has a cup of coffee ready for her.

While everyone passes out hugs, I jog down to my place. When I come back, they're still goodbye-ing. I go inside and make myself a to-go cup of coffee, too.

When I open the door to her backseat, Ivy walks over to see what I'm doing. "Is that yours?" she asks, pointing at the duffle bag I just loaded.

"Give me the keys."

"What are you doing?"

"Driving."

"All the way to the beach?"

"That's the plan."

"What about your truck?"

"Cujo's bringing it to me next week."

"What about the rest of your stuff?"

Cujo yells, "It'll be in the truck!"

Everyone looks around confused for a moment until it dawns on them what's happening, that I'm leaving now, too.

"Unless you hate this change of plans," I say, staring into Ivy's eyes, trying to gauge whether she sees this as the grand romantic gesture I intended or a massive overstep.

"I fucking love this change of plans!"

Everyone cheers like they just witnessed a successful marriage proposal. It's not that, nothing nearly so major, but it's the biggest thing I've done in a long damn time.

I lift Ivy off her feet and spin her around. She runs to get in on the passenger side as soon as I set her down. I go through my own round of handshakes and hugs, saving Petra for last.

"Good job, Romeo." She throws her arms around me. "You take care of yourself. Don't make me have to drive across two states to come kick your ass."

"I'm better than I've ever been. Thank you for everything, Petra. I owe you so much."

"Don't start that shit. Get out of here."

"You better come to my grand opening."

"Wild horses couldn't keep me away."

"So, what do you think? Is her mom going to hate me?"

"No. She's going to need a minute to adjust, but she's going to love you the moment she sees how much you love her daughter."

Ivy honks the horn, and everyone laughs. She takes a picture of them all before we drive away. She snaps one of my casita on the way out.

"Your staring chairs!" she yells.

"Cujo's bringing them."

"Okay, good. Because I really love those chairs."

"I know you do."

I drive us through the gate slowly, but I pick up speed once we're on the other side. No need to prolong anything now.

"Stop!" she yells.

I cram on the brakes. "What's wrong?"

"We have to take a picture at Bear Rock."

"You cannot scream like that when I'm behind the wheel."

"Well, if there's a photo op I don't want us to miss, and you're about to pass it, I might not have a choice."

"I will turn around and go back to it. Just don't scream like that."

"You promise? You'll go back with no complaints?"

"I didn't say anything about not complaining, but I'll go back."

"Come on. Let's take our last Ivydell pic."

I lean against the rock on one side of the bear, and she leans on the other. She takes a dozen shots before she gets one that she likes, and I know she's going to do this every time she makes me stop.

I'm still smiling when I slide back behind the wheel.

When I turn onto the highway, she says, "What are you doing? Don't you want to go to Hilltop to say goodbye to Shane?"

"We'll see plenty of Shane, trust me."

"I didn't think about that. I guess he'll want to see the winery."

"At every stage. He's actually been a great mentor for me. I'm looking forward to having him consult on it as we move forward."

"I love that we'll still get to see him. Does he know you're leaving early?"

"He knew I was going to attempt it."

"You didn't really think I'd say no, did you?"

"I wasn't sure. All I knew was that I had to try because I couldn't stand the thought of you leaving alone."

"I'm glad you took the chance."

"I'm glad you gave me a chance."

She fills her mom in on the way home, in between stops. It takes the form of many text messages and multiple phone calls. At least I'm not going to be a surprise.

If I were making this drive alone, my only stops would be for food, fuel, and bathroom breaks. Ivy finds photo ops in places and things that don't strike me as all that photogenic, but her vision is more colorful.

I keep my word and never refuse to stop. I mostly don't even complain.

It's almost dark when we get to the beach. She rolls the windows down as soon as we're close enough to smell the salt in the air. It's humid and sticky. Gulls squawk incessantly. One shits on the windshield. Ivy glows with happiness. She's home.

"Are you sure you're going to be able to live somewhere else?"

"I am more than ready to live somewhere else. But I'm a beach girl at heart. This will probably always be where I come to recharge. Can you live with that?"

"That sounds like the perfect life to me."

We're having breakfast with her mom in the morning, but for my first night in her little beach town, it's just us. She opens the door to her apartment and says, "Welcome to your temporary home."

"I didn't mean to move in on you. I'll still get my own place."

"Let's play it by ear," she says. "There's no point in you getting another place here if you're going to want to move closer to the winery once construction begins."

"That's true. Do you have plans tomorrow after we have breakfast with your mom?"

"I assumed you'd want to go see the site in person."

"You're okay with spending another day in the car?"

"It's only a few hours away. And honestly, I'm dying to see it, too."

"You want to show me your beach tonight?"

"Yes!"

We walk along the beach and talk. Some places feel instantly familiar, like it's impossible to believe you've never been there. This is one of those places.

It's the place that raised Ivy. How could I not love it here?

"Don't step on that jellyfi—"

"Shit!"

Ivy winces. "Welcome to the beach. Come on. You nursed me through my first scorpion sting. I can get you through your first jellyfish sting."

I try not to lean on her as walk back to her apartment, but fuck, this hurts. We make it inside and she leads me to the bathroom where she helps me take off my shoes and socks. "Sit on the edge of the tub."

She pours vinegar over the sting and lets it dry. Then she floods it again. After the third time, the sting actually lessens a little. She turns on the water in the tub. "You need to hold it under hot water for a while now."

"Thank God I had shoes on. At least it just got my ankle."

"Yeah, it's still going to hurt like hell for a while." She tests the water with her hand. "Stick your ankle under the running water."

I hold it there for what feels like an hour, but she swears is only thirty minutes. The sting has faded. It still hurts, but it's nothing compared to when it first happened.

We take a quick shower together. When we get out, she pats

my stung ankle dry and spreads cortisone cream over the affected area. She brings a throw pillow from her couch to the bed. "This is firmer than my pillows. It'll be good to prop your foot on."

She brings me water, and crawls into bed next to me.

"You know, when you got stung by that scorpion, I went to great lengths to take your mind off the pain."

"You did do a pretty good job of taking care of me. I'm not sure the same protocol would work for your jellyfish sting, though."

"I think we should at least try."

"You sure you feel up to doing that? I mean, if you think you can get into position. Or did you mean for me to sit on your face?"

I laugh. "You know what I meant."

She kisses my scorpion. "You think that might help, huh?"

"I'm feeling pretty sure."

She peppers kisses down my chest, continuing to my abs before she climbs between my legs. "Am I helping yet?"

"You're definitely not hurting."

Her warm sweet mouth closes over the crown of my cock. I look out over her balcony toward the waves. She has a small windchime hanging outside her bedroom, and it sounds like tiny bells when the wind blows off the water. The moonlight hits the metal and casts a flickering reflection on the glass.

Something flashes beyond her balcony, far out over the water. A shooting star, and she missed it.

"Make a wish," I say.

"What am I wishing on?"

"The shooting star I just saw."

"Are you serious? I've never seen one here."

"I saw it, and I'm telling you to make a wish."

She closes her eyes and takes a deep breath.

Who's to say two people can't wish on the same star? People share wishes all the time.

Ivy

Eighteen Months Later

"I can't believe the first wedding we're hosting is my mother's." I lean against Jensen and look out from the deck off the tasting room at Vintage Vibes. There is still construction to be completed, but this building is done. The inside isn't completely finished out, but thankfully, Mom wanted an outdoor wedding and reception.

"I'm just glad we got the grounds ready in time."

"She would've been happy to get married here, whether there was a gazebo and gardens or not." I kiss his cheek. "But thank you for everything you did to make it so nice. She cried when she saw all the Ivydell signs."

"I thought she hated that place."

"She did, but Gran didn't. And she knows it brought you and me together, and how much I loved it."

"I wish we were pouring our own wine at the reception."

"Soon," I say.

"Six more months in the barrel and we uncork the first bottle of Wild Ivy at our grand opening. Twelve more and we'll be putting up barrels from our own grapes."

"I still think we should've named our first wine after you," I say. "This whole winery was your vision."

"It never would've happened without you." He kisses my forehead. "We're going to have to tell her at some point, Ivy."

"She's softened on Ivydell, but her only daughter getting married on a whim in Vegas? No way is she hearing that until after her honeymoon."

"I thought she liked Vegas. And it's not like you married a stranger."

"She has mixed emotions when it comes to Vegas. Our news may tarnish it for good. Who I married has nothing to do with it."

"I meant it when I said I was fine with having a ceremony for our family and friends."

"And I meant it when I said that's ridiculous. We got married for us. We don't need a fancy ceremony to validate it."

"Whatever you say, Ivy Dell McAdams-Stinger."

"It's Just Ivy."

"Not a day in your life."

Mom's best friend, Maggie, runs through the tasting room toward us. She pushes open the double doors. "Ivy, hon, your Mama is in tizzy. She just realized she doesn't have something blue."

"Yes, she does. Tell her I'm on my way." I kiss my husband, and pull the sapphire pendant I commissioned from Myrna out of its box. It's set in a silver scrolled conch shell. "She'll like it, right?"

"She'll love it. Go save the day. Get ready to be the most beautiful maid of honor this place will ever see. And I'll see you at the reception."

"Save me a dance."

"You got it, wifey."

"If you ever call me that again, I'll break both your legs."

He laughs and blows me a kiss.

I smile as I walk away, wondering how I got lucky enough to have so many wishes come true.

A sparrow lands on the railing and chirps. A second flies over to join it. Jensen says they're pests and they'll leave droppings all over the deck if we don't do something to keep them off it.

I think they make the perfect wedding guests.

Bonus

Scene!

You didn't think I'd let you miss the opening of Vintage Vibes Winery, did you?

Ivy
Opening Day

I reach out from the ladder and tip an edge of the canvas ever so slightly to reposition it. It's flat against the wall, but it doesn't want to hang evenly. Not for more than a few seconds, anyway. There is no reason for it to keep tilting.

I feel Jensen behind me, watching me. Okay, I also heard him come into the tasting room and listened to his footsteps approach, and then stop.

"What do you think?" I ask.

"It's perfect."

"Finally." I step down a rung on the ladder and the canvas shifts. Dammit! Back up I go to right it again. If this were the first painting I'd hung in here, I'd be afraid we had foundation problems. Everything else stays straight and level, though, including the wine glasses hanging behind the bar.

This time, I pause after I go down a step. It holds. "I guess I'm going to have to find something to secure the edges to the wall. Hopefully, it will stay still for the opening. I descend the rest of the ladder steps.

Jensen stares at the wall and shakes his head. "I hate to tell you this, but it just moved again. I swear it's like someone's hand is pushing it, intentionally making it crooked. You might have to hang something else there."

"But I really want this painting to hang there. I'm so grateful Alma and Elma gave it to me. I want to showcase it so everyone can enjoy Gran's stormy angel."

"Maybe the angel doesn't like that spot."

No stormy angels in the deciding room. "Are you fucking kidding me?"

"It was just a thought."

"No, not you. Gran." I sigh in frustration, but it gives way to laughter. "Before we left Ivydell, Elma gave me a message from Gran that I didn't understand. She said 'no stormy angels in the deciding room.' Of course the tasting room is the deciding room! It's where people decide what they like. She doesn't want that painting there."

"Didn't you say she was always worried people might find some of her angels depressing?"

"The stormy ones. Okay, fine. It's coming down."

He squeezes my shoulders and kisses the top of my head. "I'll get it. Do you have anything else to hang there?"

"I'll swap it with Tawny's painting from my office." I walk toward the hallway, pausing to appreciate that Gran isn't knocking her windshield painting around. She must be okay with that one hanging in here, even though those raindrops are clearly meant to represent tears. It should definitely start some conversations.

Once Jensen has Tawny's painting hung in what I'd thought was the optimal spot for the stormy angel, I have to admit this is the better choice. *Thanks, Gran.*

If the message about the painting in the deciding room was real, the other things Elma predicted might've been accurate as well. I press a hand against my lower belly and wonder . . . the headache, the tiredness? But I haven't been sick, and my period's barely even late.

I've got too much to do to worry about something that might not even be happening.

"Can you move the sofa?"

"Again?" His tone is agitated, but I can't tell he's trying not to let it show. He's worked so hard for this day. I'm trying not to be too much of a pain in the ass, but I want everything to be perfect.

"Last time, I promise. I liked it better in front of the fireplace."

When Cujo brought Jensen's truck to the beach, we were both shocked to see The Spirit Sisters had sent me their deep red Victorian sofa that I'd fallen in love with. It's been in storage, waiting for the tasting room to be ready. I knew the moment I saw it on the truck that it belonged here, in a place where people will gather and share stories. It's too great a piece not to be shown off and shared.

Plus, it's another bit of Ivydell at Vintage Vibes Winery.

The final festival poster is framed, and it looks amazing. There are prints of it available in the gift shop, along with smaller prints of April's depiction of Jenzard pouring wine.

This winery is a little quirky, kind of like Ivydell, so the memorabilia and funky art are a good fit.

Petra has placed some of her soaps on consignment with us, as well as a boxed collection of her oils and tinctures.

We have some high-end merchandise, too. There is a case full of Myrna's jewelry. She created a wine-themed line just for us. It includes silver swirly wine bottles and glasses, a grape cluster, and a corkscrew, which is the one I'm wearing now. I trace it with my fingertip. My sparrow pendant will always be my favorite, but I'm smitten with this whimsical corkscrew.

She also created an amazing bottle topper. It's a scorpion, balancing a wine glass on its tail—right on the tip of its stinger. Chef's kiss.

And chocolate. We have an excellent chocolate selection.

"How's this?" Jensen asks, nodding at the sofa.

"Exactly where it belongs. Thank you."

He taps his lips, indicating words are not the thanks he expects. Laughing, I step into his arms and kiss him. "I'm glad we decided on a soft opening this evening for family and friends ahead of the public opening."

"Me, too," he says. "I can't wait to see everyone. Plus, if no one shows up when we open the doors to the public, we'll at least have friends to drown our sorrows with."

"This place is going to be packed. Everyone is all abuzz about the hot new vintner in town."

"They'll all be here to check out his gorgeous wife."

"I wish it wasn't so windy out. At least it's not raining."

"It's just a little wind," he says. "It's supposed to ease up in a little while. It'll blow the clouds away, and there will be a full moon and a sky full of stars. It's going to be a beautiful night."

My gaze scans the space from the polished bar to the huge limestone fireplace to the wall of windows looking out on the wrap-around deck. "Congratulations. You did it."

"Congratulations to us. Should we crack open a bottle early?"

"You can do whatever you want. You own this place."

He takes my hand and leads me behind the bar. I snap a few pictures of him uncorking the first bottle on opening day, and another of the initial pour. There will be an official photographer here in a few hours, but these are for me.

Jensen lifts his glass. I lift the other, and we toast to a successful opening, but I set my glass back on the bar after the first sip. "It's so good."

"If it's so good, why'd you set your glass down?"

"I'm only going to have a few sips tonight." I unconsciously glance down at my abdomen.

He sets his glass on the bar next to mine. "Do we have something else to celebrate today? Are we going to be making a big announcement at our grand opening?"

I shake my head. "It's too early to know. And even if we knew, it would be way too early to announce it. It's just a little maybe at this point, but I want to be cautious. So, just a few sips for photographs and toasts, that's all I'm having tonight."

"Just a little maybe, huh?"

His eyes go glassy, and I slap his chest. "Don't you dare! If you cry, I'll cry, and I don't have time to redo my makeup."

I look at April's mini paintings on their little easels, hoping the absurd cats will dry up my sentimental tears before they start. It works. "You look good with gray hair," I say. "You're definitely going to be a silver fox."

"And you are going to be the sexiest tattooed redhead mom ever."

My little amethyst angel ghost stares at us from between the cool cats, her mouth hanging open in awe of our secret little maybe.

Jensen's gaze shifts to the entrance, and he smiles with his whole face. I know our first guest is here.

I look over my shoulder. It's Petra, and Myrna is right behind her. I run to hug them. Jensen is right behind me.

Tawny and Leo enter next, waving bags of coffee they've brought us from somewhere new. Before the door closes, I hear Cujo's bike rumble into the lot.

I lead Petra, Myrna, Tawny and Leo around the room, excited to show them all the furniture and artwork I've chosen. Tawny's eyes mist over when she sees her painting hanging so prominently. If I'd had any doubt before, I know for sure it's in the right spot now.

They are all such a part of this, and it feels amazing to show it to them. To have so many of our Ivydell friends here for the opening of Vintage Vibes is priceless.

Cujo enters, and we all cheer and pretend to be paparazzi, snapping our invisible cameras. Basin Brotherhood just got picked up for a fourth season. The show is a huge hit, and he's sort of famous now. He had a recent incident with a photographer who didn't understand boundaries, so of course, we have to fuck with him about it.

Josephine comes in behind him, laughing at the way we're teasing Cujo over his celebrity status and his latest headlines.

Jensen beckons everyone to the bar for a toast. He's opened a second bottle of Wild Ivy and poured them all a glass. Mom walks in, hanging on her husband's arm like they're still newlyweds. She runs over to join in on the first toast, which she delays by going behind the bar to hug Jensen and tell him how proud she is of him.

He is, without a doubt, her dream son-in-law.

Zara rushes in. "I didn't miss the first toast, did I?"

"Thanks to my mom, you're just in time."

"Thanks, Mom!" she yells, running over to join us. She hugs everyone while Jensen pours her a glass of wine.

Josephine jumps up to hug her. "You heard from Dice lately?" she asks, teasingly.

"He's parking the car."

We all crack up. I already knew they had reconnected recently and were seeing each other pretty regularly, but it's news to everyone else.

Jensen shakes his head. "Well, let's wait on Dice. I am going to make a toast, eventually."

Dice comes in, looking like he's aging in reverse. I guess Miami agrees with him. Or maybe his much younger girlfriend is his fountain of youth.

Jensen lifts his glass, and we all do the same. "Thank you all for being here, but more importantly, thank you for being there. To Ivydell, the magical place that brought us all together."

"To Ivydell!" we shout.

We all take a sip in this sacred moment while we are the only ones present, just the way it was in Ivydell. Everyone compliments the wine and begins to share in turn what they've been up to lately.

Smaller conversations splinter off and then merge back into one, just like they always did when we gathered in the Community Center.

And then they come . . .

The tasting room quickly fills with the others who've been invited to the soft hours of the opening. It's mostly owners and employees of established local wineries, hotel and restaurant people from the area, and some writers from local newspapers and magazines.

There is a writer from *Texas Monthly* here, too. We weren't sure he would come, but we extended the invite, hoping the biodynamic element might pique his interest. He zeroes in on Cujo the moment he sees him. We'll be just as happy if he gets featured instead of Vintage Vibes.

Maybe we'll get lucky and the writer will toss us a mention as Cujo's friends' hippie-dippie little winery.

When the band shows up, it starts to feel very real. We own a winery.

Shane makes his entrance. He's been in town for a week, helping us with the final preparations. If anyone can hype our guests up about what we've created here, it's him. He gives us a smile and nod, and then he sidles up next to the very attractive manager of a newly opened boutique hotel and turns on his charm.

I join Jensen behind the bar. "Are you ready?"

He lifts my hand and kisses my fingers. "For this and every little maybe that comes along."

We pour wine and answer questions for our invited guests. There is a steady chorus of laughter and clinking wine glasses. By the time the public grand opening begins, my nerves are gone and I am at home in our tasting room.

Jensen watches proudly as the crowd swells. I catch his eye and smile. "Not bad for some shirtless jerk I picked up in the desert."

"It's amazing what a guy can achieve when a slutty girl from the beach throws herself at him."

We laugh and steal a kiss between pours. I whisper, "I'm pretty sure the photographer caught that."

"Good. I hope a million kisses happen in this tasting room. Hell, I don't even mind if other couples kiss sometimes, too."

The band plays. The wind gently blows. And the wine flows while a full moon rises and the big Texas sky fills with stars. Maybe someone will get a chance to wish on one before the night ends.

I hope it comes true for them.

Also from INDIE SPARKS

Steamy Rom-Com Duologies:

VENGEFUL VIXENS:
Your Boss Says Hi!

She's only looking for a rebound guy, but her ex's boss plays for keeps. He's a former NFL player who used to have thousands of women screaming his name every week. Now, he only wants one woman to scream his name, and she just might become his biggest fan yet.

Your Trainer Says Hi!

She only wants to see her ex's beloved personal trainer in the gym—until he convinces her his hot tub could do wonders for her aching muscles. He isn't wrong, but between the heat, the bubbles, and his off-the-clock skills, she might be in too deep before she knows it. He's definitely not her type. So, why can't she stop seeing him?

NAUGHTY AT THE NOUVEAU:
Maintenance & Management

She's the new property manager. He's the new maintenance supervisor. They rub each other the wrong way . . . until they start to rub each other so very right. There's a non-fraternization policy, so they really shouldn't. But there's only one bed!

Landscaping & Leasing

He ghosted her after an unfortunate incident that she had absolutely no control over—and now, she's accidentally hired his landscaping company. She may not be completely immune to his charms (that voice!), but she's not weak enough to fall for him twice. But what if she doesn't know the whole story about why he disappeared from her life?

More Small Town Romance:

Peri

They were the wildest couple in town once, but that was a long time ago. They're not restless small-town kids anymore. And she's not back in town to see him. But seeing him once won't hurt anything. How much trouble could they get into as adults? Hardly any if you disregard the dirty karaoke and the lewd (allegedly) graffiti . . . and that old flame reigniting like an inferno.